MW00942610

Cover Photo Credit - Canva, Photo-graphe from CCO, ID# MACVr8r14fk.

Scripture reference taken from The Living Bible, Tyndale House, Copyright 1971.

This book is a work of fiction. Any resemblance to actual persons, living or deceased is purely coincidental.

Table of Contents

Chapter One

Life Isn't Fair

"It isn't fair! It just isn't fair!" shouted Sarah, storming through the front door and slamming it behind her. Ranting and raving throughout the house, not even the rush of chilled air from the air-conditioner could cool her hot anger.

"Sarah, I've asked you a hundred times not to slam the door," reminded Mrs. Taylor wearily.

"If you'd heard what I just heard, you'd slam the door, too!"

"Can you put your fuming on hold until I get out of this sweaty uniform?"

Plopping down on the living room couch, Sarah muttered to herself. "I can't believe this, I just can't believe it! Of all people, why Jennifer?"

From the bedroom, her mother asked, "Pour me a glass of tea, would you? And plug in my foot massager. The hospital was a zoo today!"

Sarah peeled herself slowly off the couch and trudged to the kitchen. She wished her mother wasn't so tired in the afternoons, but at least she arrived home at the same time as she and her younger sister, Allison. Most of the other sixth-graders in her neighborhood were latch-key kids. Hearing the shower running, she took the tea to her bedroom and drank it herself, letting the sweet cool liquid travel slowly down her dry throat. Standing in front of her white hutch, Sarah wondered miserably, *why can't one of you be real?* But the only answer was silent staring from her collection of proudly displayed horse statues.

Her mother passed across the hall wrapped in a fluffy towel with her short wet hair combed back like a black bathing cap. Sarah sometimes wished she had the ease of short hair, especially during the long hot Florida summers, but whenever her mother suggested a new haircut, she cringed at the thought of not having her bouncy brown ponytail. So for the past two years, only her bangs had been trimmed.

"I'm now ready to hear what's bothering you," announced Mrs. Taylor from her recliner.

Sarah poured her mother the tea she'd asked for and carried it to the TV tray. Her anger having simmered down to self-pity, she sat dismally on the couch. "Jennifer told me on the bus today that they're getting a horse tomorrow!"

"A horse! What on earth for?"

"I'm not really sure. Jennifer just said her father and one of his law partners are buying a horse. I'm the one who's wanted a horse all my life. Jennifer doesn't care a thing about horses, and now she's getting one! She never has to save up for anything!"

After swallowing a few sips of tea, Mrs. Taylor said, "There aren't any stables nearby. Where do they plan on boarding this horse?"

"Somewhere in Grove City, I think."

"That's over an hour's drive from here. Jennifer won't be able to ride this horse very much, will she?"

"No, I guess not," Sarah admitted. "She invited me to go see him this Saturday. I bet she wants to show him off. Some best friend she is!"

"I think you should go and find out more about it before you jump to all these conclusions. It just doesn't add up. If it were that convenient, don't you think I would have looked into getting you a horse of your own? Remember how far you had to drive when Grandma got you those riding lessons last summer?"

"It was a long drive," agreed Sarah. "How long have I actually wanted a horse, anyway?"

"Well, let's see. You first wanted a pony when you were three, and we took you to the fair."

Sarah smiled. She didn't remember, but there were lots of pictures of that special day.

"After six pony rides, we couldn't drag you off! Your chubby little fingers were wrapped around the saddle horn so tightly. I finally bribed you off with some pink and green cotton candy." Mrs. Taylor laughed at the memory. "And then at Jerry Rinaldi's fifth birthday party, you rode a big horse. What a great time you had that day! You must have ridden that old plow horse ten times around the yard. Jerry's grandfather was so nice and patient, remember?"

Now Sarah laughed. She did remember that day when Jerry had his party at his grandfather's farm. "Where was that farm?"

"It was near Grove City, as I recall."

"I guess I'll check it out," said Sarah sheepishly.

"Good, because I want to hear all about this mystery horse when you get home!"

* * *

Early Saturday morning, Sarah tapped on the Gibson's back door. No kid ever used the front door because Mrs. Gibson's living room rug was vanilla white, which she could never understand. How was it possible for a normal family to live in a house with white carpet? Jennifer and her pesky little brother, Mike, were only allowed in the living room to practice their piano lessons (in their stocking feet) and when they had company. They didn't have any dogs or cats due to the families' allergies. Sarah always thought it was pretty strange that the whole Gibson family was allergic to animal hair. (Jennifer never sneezed at her house). But the craziest thing was that when she and Jennifer first became friends, Jennifer wasn't allowed to get dirty. But all that changed when they became best friends. Between the shallow sandy creek behind Sarah's house, her menagerie of rabbits, rats, mice, a cat and a dog, and her intrigue with interesting trash piles, Mrs. Gibson finally gave up trying to keep Jennifer clean and was grateful just to have her daughter come home in one piece! So it didn't make much sense that a family with white carpeting and allergies would go off and buy a horse.

Mike, who was in the same third grade class as Allison, answered the door wearing his silly, too small cowboy outfit from last Halloween. "Hi, Mike. Isn't it a little early for Halloween?" she sneered sarcastically.

"Mom," whined Mike, "Sarah's teasing me."

"Mom, Sarah's teasing me…" echoed Jennifer. "Quit being such a baby, Mike."

"Is he going dressed like that?" Sarah hoped not.

"Unfortunately, yes. I tried to tell my mother he was going to embarrass us, but she thinks he's cute."

"I don't know which is worse. A tag-a-long sister who's a copycat or a goofy little brother who thinks he's everyone but himself!" said Sarah shaking her head.

"Everyone ready?" chimed Mrs. Gibson. "Before we go, I want everyone to tinkle one more time."

"Mother, please!" groaned Jennifer. "Or a mother who thinks you're still three!" giggled Jennifer as the traipsed down the hall.

Even though it was early April, the Florida sun shone through the car windows with a vengeance. Sarah hated the way her sweaty thighs stuck to the leather seats in the Gibson's car and much preferred her mother's rusty old station wagon with its colorfully stained cloth seats. Jennifer and Mike weren't allowed to text, listen to music with their ear buds, or watch movies in their mother's car. How boring just to sit "and look at the scenery" as Mrs. Gibson liked to say. And the music she listened to on the radio! It knocked a person out like a tranquilizer. Thank goodness, Sarah had her smart phone! They could at least play games with that.

Two hours later, sprawling live oaks with octopus limbs and jagged beards of Spanish moss replaced the towering downtown skyscrapers of Tampa. Sparse sandy pastures lined the freeway, leaving the congested city behind and soon, acres of leafy green orange groves lined the landscape like rows of sturdy soldiers.

Sarah was aching to ask Mrs. Gibson all kinds of questions, but now she was listening to a dull talk radio show about household cleaning hints and the stain-removing power of vinegar, of all things. All Sarah knew about vinegar was that the pungent smell made her eyes water and the taste of it ruined a perfectly good potato salad.

Yawning for the hundredth time, she tuned out the radio and soon succumbed to the lulling drone of the wheels and warmth penetrating through the rear window. A bumpy country road roused her from her nap, and she awoke with a start. Wiping the drool away from the side of her mouth, she eagerly watched out the window like an excited dog with his nose pressed against the pane. Mrs. Gibson turned down a long secluded dirt drive where a cheerfully painted sign welcomed them to the Sunshine Stables. As soon as they parked, she jumped out of the car, fascinated with the small but tidy farm. To the left was a training track and bright white barn with green trim. Behind and to the right, scattered among the shady oaks and tall pines were a dozen or so grazing Thoroughbreds. Sarah was smitten with their arching elegant necks and long delicate legs. There were bays and browns, but the horse that caught her eye and nearly took her breath away was the jet-black one whose coat shone like a raven's brilliant wings. "Which one is yours," she asked Jennifer wistfully.

"The black one," replied Jennifer, nonchalantly.

Sarah decided she was going to die right then and there. But then Mike ran up, swinging a rope wildly around, almost knocking everyone's eye out, so dying would have to wait until later. Ducking, she shielded her face from the whirling, spinning weapon. Dying was one thing, going blind was quite another.

"Mike, stop waving that rope. You're going to scare the horses," scolded Jennifer.

But it was too late. A dozen or so heads went up; all ears perked forward, then all turned and ambled away from the minor annoyance.

"Now see what you did!" barked Jennifer.

"Yeah, thanks a lot, Mike," added Sarah coldly.

"This is boring," he complained. Impatient for action, he went to investigate the barn, while the girls tried to coax the herd back to the fence.

As Sarah gazed at the beautiful black horse, jealous feelings started to sprout like weeds after a summer rain. Jennifer was petrified of large dogs and wouldn't even pet the friendliest canines in the neighborhood. *There's no way she's gonna ride that horse!* Sighing wearily, she knew deep down it was useless and stupid to hold a grudge. Before her envy could take root, she turned away and trudged back to the barn.

"Can we ride him?" she asked Mrs. Gibson hopefully.

"This horse isn't for pleasure riding, Sarah," explained Mrs. Gibson.

"He's for racing!" interrupted the trainer enthusiastically.

"He's a racehorse?" She didn't know whether to feel disappointment or relief.

"We have high hopes for him. Both his sire and dam were proven winners," the trainer said proudly.

"What's his name?" asked Jennifer.

"We call him Tuffy, but his registered mane is Mr. Tough Stuff."

Mrs. Gibson took a few photographs of Tuffy with her phone and then it was time to go.

"Can't we stay a little longer?" pleaded Mike.

"You said you were bored," reminded Jennifer.

For once, Sarah agreed with Mike. Maybe there was another horse around here she could ride.

"No, I have to get back for my hair appointment," said Mrs. Gibson, glancing at her watch.

"Can't your hair wait?" persisted Mike

"No, because your father and I have a dinner engagement tonight," she said matter-of-factly. "Now come along and we'll stop for a hamburger on the way home."

"Yes!" Mike raced to the car, his clumsy cowboy boots kicking up the gray sandy dirt.

Sarah walked back to the car frustrated and annoyed. *What a waste of time!* There was one thing to be glad about however; the beautiful black horse was only a business investment.

Thankfully, the ride home went faster. (It always did, for some reason.) After a quick lunch, she felt more like her old self again, as she and Jennifer planned their afternoon escapades.

*   *   *

"So tell me about Jennifer's new horse," said Mrs. Taylor, as she dressed for dinner that evening.

"I've never seen such a good-looking horse in my entire life," said Sarah dreamily.

"Did you get to ride him?" asked her mother, her eyes opened wide as she applied mascara.

"No, because he's training to be a racehorse."

"I knew there had to be a reasonable explanation." The words were garbled as she traced her open lips with a crimson-colored lipstick.

"Where are you and David going tonight?"

"There's a new Italian place near the university we thought we'd try."

"Will you be late?"

"Aren't we always?" teased her mother. One eye was closed now for a touch more eyeshadow.

"How late can I stay up?"

"Well, I guess you can stay up until eleven. Here, help me put on this bracelet."

"Didn't Dad give you this bracelet?" Somehow, it didn't seem right wearing her father's gift on a date with David.

Mrs. Taylor murmured quietly, admiring the simple but elegant gold chain. "Yes, he gave this to me on the night you were born. I remembered he apologized because he wanted it to be a diamond, but that was a luxury we couldn't afford. I told him no diamond could match the precious jewel I held in my arms." Her voice quivered slightly, but she erased the pain with a sigh and a smile.

"Do you think you should wear it tonight?"

"Your father would want me to wear it."

"How do you know?"

"Because he told me so."

"What did he say?"

"A few hours before he died, he suddenly had a lot of energy – that happens sometimes, you know. And he talked and talked. About you girls, about us and our lives without him.

"He knew he was going to die?" Sarah realized there was much she didn't know about her dad and that tragic night.

"Many people do," said her mother softly.

"What else did he say?"

"He wanted us to remember him and love him, but he also wanted us to live our lives to the fullest."

"What did he mean by that?" asked Sarah, who could scarcely believe that nearly two years had gone by since that horrible rainy night when her father's car had been hit head-on by a drunk driver.

"For me, it means that your father hoped I would re-marry one day – if I wanted to. Basically, he didn't want any of us to stop loving."

"Are you and David going to get married?" There. She finally asked the question that had been plaguing her mind for months.

Mrs. Taylor paused a moment before answering. "We're thinking about it." She paused again. "You know, Sarah, the human heart has enough room to love more than just one person."

"I don't know, Mom," mumbled Sarah, now stretched across her mother's bed.

"David is very fond of you and Allison," she added. "You know that, don't you?"

"I guess so." She stared at the ceiling fan, wishing the drunk driver had died instead of her father.

The first year had been really hard. The accident happened in early June, and she remembered how relieved she was that she didn't have to go to school. It would have been impossible to concentrate on her lessons with everybody staring and whispering about her dead father. She and her mother had cried a lot, sometimes together, but mostly alone in their beds at night. Then she and Allison went to stay with their grandmother for a few weeks while Mrs. Taylor traveled to North Carolina to visit their father's relatives.

When her mom returned, she took a few weeks off work to be by herself, then decided it was best to return to her nursing job at the hospital. "When I'm busy helping others, my own pain doesn't feel quite as sharp," she had explained to Grandma, who thought her daughter needed more time to grieve.

The doorbell rang.

"I'll get it," sang Allison, who adored David.

Sometimes Sarah envied her little sister, who had just turned six when their dad died. And although Allison missed her daddy very much, she eagerly accepted David right from the start.

"How's my girl?" cooed David, picking Allison up and twirling around the room as she squealed with delight.

"How's it going, Sarah?" He smiled warmly and gave her the kind of hug a visiting uncle gives – *I'm glad to see you, but I know you're a little shy*, side embrace.

"Fine," answered Sarah coolly. She wasn't quite sure what she thought of David now that she knew *they* were "thinking about marriage," so she slid onto the couch like a snake and re-coiled herself in the safety of the television. It was true she liked David. He was easy to talk to and liked to do fun things with them, like the giant waterslide and the rollercoasters at the state fair. And he was nice-looking. He had dark wavy hair and big blue eyes that seemed to light up any room he entered. But what kind of stepfather would he be? He didn't have any kids of his own, so he didn't have any experience, which could be good or bad. Would he be overly strict? Or maybe he'd try too hard to be a perfect father and drive everyone crazy. Or maybe he wouldn't care that much once they were married. The possibilities were endless.

"Will you bring me a doggie bag, Uncle David?" asked Allison, bouncing on the couch.

"No promises but I'll try."

"Really all I want is some dessert," she flirted from behind her cat green eyes.

"I sort of figured that," winked David, who knew only too well how important dessert was to Allison. She had tried for many years to weasel a dessert after breakfast, but had recently given up trying. Mrs. Taylor had been as unwavering as a giant rock formation and it had finally paid off.

"Oh, brother," moaned Sarah, slapping her forehead and rolling her eyes back in mock aggravation. "Every Saturday night, you two have this same conversation!"

"So what?" chirped Allison.

"We've started a new tradition, that's all," chuckled David.

"It's driving me crazy!" Sarah covered her head with the couch pillow.

"Want me to call the funny farm?" asked David, with a goofy grin.

"Ha-Ha. Just make sure you bring me some dessert, too!" she laughed.

"Consider it done!" Then turning his attention to Mrs. Taylor, who had just entered the room, he said dreamily, "Amy, you look absolutely ravishing!"

"Thank-you, David. You look rather handsome, yourself."

Sarah smiled. It was nice to see her mother happy and pretty again. For too long she had just gotten by with the essentials. No make-up, jewelry or matching accessories. "I feel like a part of me has died," she had confided to Sarah, "and I just want to blend in without anyone noticing." But David had noticed. After a year had gone by, David, who was a professor of philosophy at the university, collapsed during one of his lectures and was rushed to the hospital for an emergency appendectomy where Mrs. Taylor was his nurse. It wasn't love at first sight, but they enjoyed each other's company so much, she would return to the hospital after work to visit him. And when David was well, he called and asked her out. They had been dating for almost a year, and now Sarah's recent suspicions had just been confirmed by her mother.

Meanwhile Allison, who already had her own wedding planned, relished all this romance while Sarah pretended not to hear.

"Grandma's here" she announced, when the doorbell rang.

"Sarah, don't forget to help Grandma with dinner," reminded her mother.

"And don't forget, it's your turn to do the dishes!" quipped Allison.

"I wish we had a dishwasher."

"We have two fine dishwashers in this house. Why should I go out and buy another one?" joked Mrs. Taylor. "Hello, Mom."

"Hello everybody. Sorry I'm a little late. That traffic seems to get heavier and slower every week."

"So I guess I'm stuck with dishpan hands for the rest of my life." Sarah tried once more as her mom gave her swift kiss good-bye."

"Looks that way." Like a statue, her mother was again unmoved.

"Have a good time!" Grandma followed them out, waving good-bye until the car had turned from sight.

"Grandma, why do you stand there and wave so long?" inquired Allison.

"I must have picked that up from my mother. The men in our family were always going off to one war or another, and we always waved until the bus or train was out of sight."

"Why?" asked Allison, who still wasn't satisfied.

"Because," said Grandma quietly, "we didn't know if they were coming home or not."

"Oh," said Allison, now content with the explanation. Then she wondered aloud,

"I wonder what kind of dessert David will bring me."

Chapter Two

The Dream

As Sarah prepared for bed that night, images of Jennifer's black beauty ran wild and free through her imagination. Climbing into bed, she mumbled to herself, "Race horse or not, I bet I could ride Mr. Tough Stuff, no problem." Before drifting off to sleep, she saw herself taming and mounting the unbroken colt with a firm but loving hand. Later on, after falling into a deep sleep, her thoughts formed a dream so vivid, it seemed real. An ebony colt, just like Jennifer's, lived in the backyard without a fence or rope to keep him from running away. Sarah loved her colt and spent every spare minute with him, brushing him daily until his coat shone like expensive black marble, and his magnificent mane and tail flowed like thick molten lava. She brought him crunchy orange carrot sticks and fresh juicy apples, making his coal black eyes sparkle like two black gems, as he gobbled up the delicious treats!

Sarah rode her dream horse throughout the neighborhood without a saddle or bridle for control, since he went willingly wherever she asked him to go. She felt like a princess when he pranced and strutted for all to see and admire and was the envy of all the children on the block, for only she could ride the stormy colt. For anyone else, he was wild and ferocious with his nostrils flaring and hooves flying.

"Sarah, time to get up," called her mother from the kitchen.

She fought waking up. *No, let me stay with him, Mom,* her mind begged.

"Sarah, wake up," said Mrs. Taylor, shaking her gently. "It's time to get ready for church."

Slowly, Sarah opened her eyes and mumbled, "I have to feed my horse first."

"What horse?" asked Mrs. Taylor, her dark eyebrows arching in surprise through her cream-covered beauty mask.

"My stallion in the backyard," insisted Sarah, now fully awake. Throwing her covers to one side, she bounced out of bed, hurried to the window and pushed aside the blue gingham curtains. The colt, who had been there only minutes before, was nowhere in sight. She stood staring at the empty yard feeling certain this had been no dream. *But it must have been,* she silently reasoned. As the truth of reality sank deeper and deeper, the burden of disappointment grew heavier.

"That must have been some dream you had." Her mother stood beside her looking out the window. Giving her a light kiss on the forehead she said, "You can tell us about it at breakfast. Hurry now or we'll be late."

In a daze, Sarah methodically selected her blue jean skirt and a blue-green blouse with orange and yellow flowers that Grandma had brought her last fall from her trip to Hawaii. She wasn't sure if they matched or not, and she really didn't care. Never in her life had she confused a dream with real life. But for a fleeting moment in time, as she lay in bed that morning, still half-asleep, her mind had traveled to another dimension; another world in a different place that was as real as the horseless world to which she had returned. Like a persistent door-to-door salesman, the dream knocked at the entrance of her mind all day long. During Sunday school, the lesson bounced over her head like a hard rubber ball. Unlike her mother, her friends wouldn't understand this strange wonderful event so she kept it to herself, hoping the nameless colt would visit her again.

At the dinner table that evening, Mrs. Taylor said quietly, "We need to have a talk, girls."

"Is this talk the reason David's not eating with us tonight?' asked Sarah suspiciously. Since David loved to cook, he spent many evenings in their kitchen whipping up mostly good meals. A few were too exotic for Sarah and Allison's undeveloped taste buds and on those nights, a pizza suited them just fine. But this Sunday evening, he was noticeably absent.

"As a matter of fact, it is." Mrs. Taylor finished her last bite of tuna casserole, then pushed her plate off to one side.

"Did David propose to you last night?" she asked, recalling their conversation from the night before.

"We've been talking about getting married, but it was something we weren't going to rush into. I think we're both a little scared." Her mother smiled and blushed simultaneously.

"So what's the big secret?" asked Sarah, trying to sound casual while the tuna casserole formed a knot of noodles in the pit of her stomach.

"David's been offered a teaching position at another school in another state."

"So, you want to marry David right away, is that it?" She didn't need a news flash to confirm the latest development.

"That's it."

"And then we all move away to this other state and live happily ever after?"

"In a nutshell, yes."

Allison, who didn't seem the least bit bothered by this momentous announcement, paused briefly from slurping her cherry jello to ask, "Where is the other school?"

"It's in a small town in Kentucky."

"Kentucky! That's kind of far from here isn't it?" exclaimed Sarah.

"It's a couple days drive."

"Why does David want to leave the university?"

"For several reasons. The college in Kentucky is offering him the head of the philosophy department. Also, David grew up in a small town, and he'd like to live in one again. And frankly, that idea appeals to me, too. This city is bursting at the seams, and I think a change would be good for all of us." Mrs. Taylor caught her breath. "So what do you two think?"

"Does it matter?" groused Sarah, who truly didn't know what to think.

"It's okay with me," said Allison indifferently. "Can I have my dessert now?"

"The jello was your dessert."

"That was my fruit," insisted Allison. "Can I have a popsicle?"

"Yes, but take it outside."

Allison ran to the freezer to make her important selection, then trundled out the backdoor.

"To answer your question," said her mother, turning to Sarah, "yes, it does matter. Very much. It's been hard on both of us since Daddy died, and just as things are finally starting to settle down, I'm asking you to make another big adjustment. But Sarah, I love David, and he doesn't want to be apart from us. And he has to give the college his answer by this Wednesday."

"What about Grandma?" She asked, her voice faltering.

"She can visit us as often and for as long as she likes," her mom soothed.

An awkward silence passed, but deep down, Sarah understood her mother's feelings.

"David's bringing a DVD over this evening to show us the area," she added. "He should be here any minute. Are you going to be all right?"

Sarah nodded that she was and got up to clear the table. Her mother took the plates from her and set them back on the table. Giving her a long hug, she whispered, "Your Dad would be real proud of you."

The girls were in their bedrooms when David arrived. Sarah didn't know whether to shout "congratulations" or "bon voyage" and felt sheltered staying in her room. Allison kept knocking on her door announcing his arrival, which she chose to ignore.

"Allison, leave your sister alone," she overheard her mother say. "Come help me pop some popcorn."

"Oh, boy! Popcorn!" she exclaimed, skipping down the hall.

While her mother and sister were busy in the kitchen, Sarah cautiously ventured into the living room like a cat on the prowl. She watched glumly from her curled position on the couch as David inserted the DVD. For the first time since she had known David, he looked nervous and out-of-place as he fumbled with the television.

"Why don't we just look at their website? It would be easier," she mumbled.

"This is from a friend of mine. We'll check out the website, too." said David, smiling weakly. "I think you'll like living in Wilmore. It's nestled right in the heart of the bluegrass country."

The word bluegrass caught Sarah's attention. "Isn't that where the racehorses are raised?"

"They sure are," David said encouragingly.

"Popcorn, anyone?" Mrs. Taylor passed around bowls of fluffy white popcorn while David pulled up the first image.

"Lights! Camera! Action!" he joked, flipping the light switch.

"Oh, how pretty!" remarked her mom. "Isn't that pretty, Sarah?"

"Yeah, it's pretty," she admitted. The pastoral farm scene of rolling green hills with rows of tall corn and acres of freshly cut hay were much more appealing than the flat Florida scrub.

The next scene was the campus lawn buried under a carpet of glistening white snow. It definitely didn't resemble the warm sunny Gulf beaches that Sarah was accustomed to.

"Snow!" screeched Alison. "Can we build snowmen and go sledding, Uncle David?"

Sarah muffled a melodramatic groan. At the rate she was going, Allison would have her suitcase packed and ready to go before school tomorrow.

"Sure, we can do all that stuff!" answered David enthusiastically.

"That sounds like fun. Doesn't that sound like fun, Sarah?" coaxed her mom.

"Yeah, I guess so," she answered with an exasperated sigh. The dark desolate trees of winter with their skeletal limbs clawing the cloudy gray sky made her shiver as she compared this scene to the smooth glassy Gulf of Mexico in the calm early morning hours. She loved that tranquil time on the beach when the sun-worshippers, jet-skiers and skim-boarders were not yet a part of this serene setting, and the only sounds that reached her ears as she scavenged for shells, starfish and other nautical treasures were the distant cries of hungry sea gulls and the rhythmic lapping of waves just waking up.

Occasionally, an early morning jogger passed by, smiling through their panting or nodding a brief hello or there might be another wandering treasure-seeker, usually an older woman with a plastic-handled grocery bag, stooping over to examine a potential prize with hopes of adding it to her bathroom shelf of collectibles or framing a hall mirror.

The beach was less than an hour away and in that short time, she felt herself transported to a different world with sleek sailboats skimming across the sea, their sails billowing against a cloudless blue backdrop, while pale green sea oats beckoned in the breeze from their comfortable seats in the soft deep sand. Then the fishermen arrived. Old men with thinning fly-away hair, leathery brown skin and stained tattered shorts carried their buckets, nets and poles to shore and set up shop until noon, returning again in the evening to repeat the routine after the harsh mid-day sun had waned in the west. While the old men studied and compared each other's haul, Sarah, Allison and frequently Jennifer, made a game of running and ducking under the taut fishing lines stretched from poles buried in the hard-washed shore.

Sometimes, they'd stay the whole day and watch the sunset – a different lightshow every night with an original cast of clouds making their debut performance, and always ending with the star of the show exiting behind the curtain of a vast endless sea. Now the beach would be a part of her past – and out of reach.

A new scene of a nearby horse farm abruptly replaced the mesmerizing seascape. Before her stood stately red and white gabled barns secluded behind miles of neat white fences. Between the barns and the fence grazed dozens of bronze-colored mares with their spring foals lingering near their mother's protective shadow.

Sarah barely noticed the remaining pictures. They weren't important- just photos of the college facilities, some local historical landmarks, available housing and of course, the local schools. Like a piece of food stuck between her teeth, the image of the majestic horse farm and the rolling countryside was wedged in her brain. Suddenly, in the darkness of the living room, a light bulb flickered in her mind. This could be the chance she'd been waiting and hoping for all her life – to finally get a horse of her own!

Like a pot of boiling water, the mares and foals dissipated from view as the faraway sound of David's voice suddenly penetrated her ears. "What do you think of Kentucky?" he asked, while her mother turned on the lights.

"I like the snow!" cried Allison, jumping off the couch. "I want to build a snow fort and throw snowballs," she declared, somersaulting across the sofa until her grubby unwashed feet landed in Sarah's lap.

"What about you, Sarah?" asked her mother.

Shoving the perpetually dirty feet from her lap with a look of big sister scorn, she slowly revealed a sly smile, and then chirped, "When's the wedding?"

* * *

A whirlwind wedding took place in three short weeks. It all seemed a bit rushed, but there was much work to be done and no time to spare. A large *For Sale* sign was erected in the front yard, and Sarah and Allison found themselves relegated to frequent mowing and weed-pulling. Years of living had to be sorted through from the attic to the storage room before being packed and delivered to Wilmore by the end of May. Exasperated and sweating profusely, Mrs. Taylor wiped away the steady beads of sweat from her forehead and upper lip and announced, "We are having a *major* garage sale!"

Between mowing and sorting, Sarah scoured the neighborhood in search of new homes for her menagerie of hamsters, rats, and rabbits that lounged lazily in their cages, oblivious to the hectic activity surrounding them. Asking Jennifer was out of the question, but she had good luck with a family down the street made up of five boys and one baby daughter. They happily accepted the entire lot, adding it to their already overcrowded backyard.

The wedding was a simple, relaxed affair held in Grandma's large shady backyard. The invitations were sent by word-of-mouth, a friend videotaped the ceremony and absolutely no gifts were permitted! "I will absolutely croak if I have to deal with wedding gifts and thank-you notes on top of everything else," her mother had proclaimed. Instead, everyone brought a generous pot-luck dish, card tables, chairs and blankets for the kids. As bridesmaids, Sarah and Allison accompanied their mother down the grassy aisle with fresh home-made bouquets picked from Grandma's ample flower garden that morning. They wore their Sunday best and

Mrs. Taylor looked stunning in her newly purchased peach chiffon dress accented with delicate lace around the collar.

David's out-of-town brother, and his best friend served as best man and groomsman. Sarah felt totally embarrassed being escorted back down the aisle after the ceremony with a six-foot handsome stranger! She was surprised to see so many guests who came on such short notice and who brought so much food. Jennifer had a seat facing the aisle and attempted to sneak a picture of Sarah as she tried in vain to walk slowly and gracefully in her stiff pumps, but all she got was a photo of a pair of fuzzy scraped up knees!

Three picnic tables were laden with everything from fried chicken to finger sandwiches to peach cobbler and cream-filled éclairs. Sarah had been too excited to eat much breakfast, and it was all she could do to keep from drooling all over herself while the vows were exchanged. After a few photographs were taken, she dashed to the guest bedroom and changed into a short set her mother had pre-approved before feasting on the bountiful array. As she and Jennifer ate under the shade of a spreading live oak, Jennifer said with her mouth full of pudding, "Your mom's not Mrs. Taylor anymore. Isn't that weird?"

"Yeah, she's Mrs. Conner, now." Sarah swallowed a twinge of sadness along with a miniature meatball. "But Taylor is her new middle name," she explained.

"Oh," said Jennifer. "That's a good idea."

Sarah thought so, too. This way, her father's name wasn't just tossed carelessly aside as if he never existed. It was to remain an important part of their life, much to Sarah's relief.

Both girls pigged-out until they felt like a couple of swollen ticks about to pop. Sarah had tried to save room for some wedding cake, but it was hopeless. There wasn't an ounce of space left in her distended belly. "I'll just have to wait until after dinner tonight," she reasoned contentedly.

It had been arranged that Sarah and Allison would spend a few days with their grandmother while Mr. and Mrs. Conner spent their short honeymoon house-hunting in Wilmore. "I'm going to miss my two favorite grand-daughters so much," she lamented, giving them extra kisses on their foreheads as she tucked them into the twin guest beds that night.

"But, Grandma, we're your only grand-daughters!" said Allison with a long wide yawn.

"I know and that's why you're my favorites!" she winked.

Sarah knew the smile on Grandma's face was a mask, trying to cover her real sadness. "When are you coming up to visit us?" she asked, trying not to get choked up. Sarah loved her grandmother dearly and horse or no horse, she was beginning to have serious doubts about this new arrangement.

"I'll be up before you know it," she reassured in a hushed whisper as Allison quickly drifted off to sleep.

"Grandma, I was wondering something," whispered Sarah reluctantly.

"What is it, dear?" Grandma motioned for Sarah to follow her into her bedroom.

Sinking into the overstuffed easy chair she stammered, "Do you think David expects me to call him *Dad* from now on?"

"Have you talked to your mother about this?" asked Grandma, sitting on the edge of her bed and slipping off her shoes.

"It's been so busy at our house, I haven't had a chance."

"I think David would want you to call him whatever you're comfortable with," she said, sitting down at her large oak vanity, dabbing her face with white dots of moisturizer.

"I feel so funny around him lately," she confessed.

"Well, that's only natural. Think how nervous he must feel suddenly having two daughters in the third and sixth grades. Most new fathers have a little more head start!" chuckled Grandma, smearing the white dots into her round cherubic face.

"Allison started calling him 'Daddy-David' as soon as they decided to get married. And it seemed so easy for her, like it was no big deal at all," she said almost resentfully.

"Sometimes changes are easier for youngsters." Grandma rose and walked to the back of the easy chair where she stroked Sarah's shiny brown hair. "After all, you have a lot more memories to contend with." Her voice was soft and soothing like baby powder on a prickly heat rash.

The long eventful day was catching up with Sarah, and the more her eyelids drooped, the less she was able to think. "I'm tired of thinking about it," she yawned.

"You'll feel better in the morning," comforted Grandma as she guided her worn-out grand-daughter back to her waiting bed.

Grandma was right. Sarah did feel better the next morning. It was Sunday and everyone slept late. When she woke up, her thoughts picked up from where they left off the night before. Sometime during her sleep, she must have decided to continue calling David, David because it immediately seemed the sensible thing to do. After all, it wasn't like she had taken any vows or exchanged rings. Now that this topic was settled, Sarah could start thinking about other, more important things; like David moving in with them when he and her mother returned on Wednesday.

The next evening, while Sarah was doing her math homework, her mother called, sounding exuberant. "Oh, Sarah, it's so pretty up here! The weather's still cool and there's spring flowers everywhere- even the trees and shrubs are blooming. You know, having lived all my life in Florida,

I never realized there was such a rainbow of colors in nature!" Her mother's voice was breathless with excitement. "And we found a nice old house with a big front porch and a swing. And guess what? Your bedrooms are in the attic!"

"The attic! What's so wonderful about that?" asked Sarah, horrified at the thought of a dark musty attic crawling with spiders, roaches and maybe even a bat or two clinging to the rafters.

"I know what you're thinking and it's not like that at all, I promise. It's really neat. The attic was converted into bedrooms and there's tons of room. The only difference is the slanted ceiling."

"Won't we be bumping our heads all the time?"

"Not if we arrange your furniture right. We'll put your bed near the slant and it will be so cozy!"

Sarah couldn't remember the last time her mother was this enthusiastic about anything so rather than being a stick in the mud, she put her reservations on hold until she could judge this room for herself.

On Wednesday evening, "the Conners" were due home. Sarah felt like a scared mouse darting about its cage while a bored house cat peered in, licking its chops. She tried reading, watching TV and calling Jennifer. She even tried doing her homework, but nothing worked. Her mind was obsessed with one persistent question: What would it be like having David live with them? He had already moved his belongings over which hadn't taken very long since he was a bachelor renting a furnished apartment. Already, his presence was clearly felt as Sarah wandered into the master bedroom and opened the closet door. His clothes were hanging where her father's used to hang and his shoes sat in the same spot as her father's shoes. *This is too weird! What if his personality has changed? What if he's suddenly mean and bossy and all this being nice was just an act?* She'd heard horror stories at school and up until now, it had been easy to ignore them. She didn't open the dresser drawers- that would be rude- but she knew his shirts and shorts were tucked in there along with his socks and underwear. Stacked against one wall were boxes of books and papers waiting to be moved to their new home in an old house in Kentucky. "Guess I can't wander around in my underwear anymore," she said to herself dismally.

Suddenly from the living room was a squeal of delight. *Honestly, that kid sounds like a baby pig,* thought Sarah, ambling out into the commotion, where Mr. and Mrs. Conner made their entrance bearing gifts like the Three Wise Men (minus one). Allison's eyes were aglow and her mouth was open wide enough for a fly to zoom in as David presented her with the latest Barbie doll to hit the shelves. "And it's not even Christmas or my birthday or anything," she gasped in awe, ripping the perfectly ravishing doll from her plastic cocoon.

"Her days as a beauty queen are over," joked Sarah as she watched her sister experiment with different hairstyles on the helpless doll.

"Ain't that the truth," laughed Mrs. Conner. Turning to David, she said, "You should see all the ravaged creatures lying in the toy box who suffered at the hands of my youngest here."

"Yeah, Allison's toy box is more like a coffin full of dead dolls!" Sarah laughed like a vampire.

"I can't wait!" chuckled David. "But before we go any further…" David presented Sarah with a beautiful life-like thoroughbred horse statue to add to her collection, and her mother gave her a colorful book on Kentucky thoroughbreds full of bright glossy photographs. Now it was Sarah's turn to let a fly zoom into her mouth.

"Thanks Mom and Da…" She started to say Dad, out of habit, she guessed, but caught herself in time, "and David, this is really nice."

"You're very welcome. Your mom and I thought you'd enjoy reading up on Kentucky's claim to fame," replied David warmly.

Grandma got a big box of famous chocolates, handmade on the Kentucky side of the Ohio River and a hand woven rug crafted by Appalachian college students. "These are wonderful! Oh, you'll have to send me more as soon as you arrive. My goodness, they just melt in your mouth," she exclaimed. Grandma loved expensive chocolate and considered herself quite a connoisseur when it came to fine candy.

"It'll be first on our *to do* list," chuckled David.

Sarah glanced up from her book, eyeing him. He seemed more relaxed, more like his old self, which in turn, made her feel a little more comfortable. And her mom, well, radiant was the word that came to mind watching her mother smile and laugh so easily, like she had been before the accident. It was late and being a school night, Sarah and Allison headed to bed. While David read Allison a short bedtime story, Mrs. Conner sat with Sarah who was still leafing through her new book.

"So how was everything while we were gone?" she asked.

"Fine," answered Sarah honestly, since nothing out of the ordinary had occurred.

"How'd you do on your math test?"

"I got a B. Did you see any kids in our new neighborhood?"

"A few."

"Did they look nice?"

"As far as I could tell."

"Mom, I'm getting really nervous about leaving. I won't have a best friend anymore. Jennifer wishes we'd stay here, ya know."

"I know. There are things about moving that are fun and hard at the same time. You and Jennifer can text and call each other, and you can see her when you go visit Grandma."

"There's one more thing." She hesitated.

"You can tell me, Sarah."

"I want to keep calling David, David. I just can't call him Dad," she sputtered.

"That's perfectly all right. But if you ever feel like calling him Dad one day, I know he'd like that."

"I do like him," she added as an afterthought.

"I know you do, and he's very fond of you. He'd like to come say good-night."

"Okay." She rolled over and turned off her bedside lamp.

David wandered in as Mrs. Conner kissed her daughter good-night. "Sweet dreams," she said softly.

"And don't let the bed bugs bite!" added David cheerfully, leaning over to give Sarah a peck on her cheek.

"Oh, brother!" she giggled, pulling the covers over her head.

Chapter Three

Moving Day

The highly publicized Conner-Taylor garage sale was held on the first Saturday in May, which coincided with the most celebrated day in Kentucky, "the run for the roses," otherwise known as Derby Day! In honor of this historic horse race, (and another recent romantic event) David surprised his new bride and step-daughters with a dozen red roses at breakfast.

"Oh, David. They're beautiful!" exclaimed Mrs. Conner, inhaling the delicate fragrance. "But what's the occasion?"

"Today's the Kentucky Derby, and it's our second week anniversary as a family," chirped David.

"You are just too sweet," she cooed, as they kissed and nuzzled.

All this early morning cheerfulness and mushy romance made Sarah squeamish. "Hey, you two. Some people are trying to eat around here, if you don't mind." A milk trail dribbled down her chin as she slurped the last of her soggy cereal.

"I like it!" piped up Allison, as she fixed herself a bagel.

"Sarah's never been much of a morning person," explained her mother. "What I have to go through to wake her up..."

"Like waking up a grumpy old bear that's been hibernating all winter!" offered Allison.

"That pretty well sums it up," smiled Mrs. Conner.

"With all this smooching and cuddling going on, it's a wonder we're even having this garage sale!" Sarah liked to pretend all this romance bothered her, but deep down, she had to admit it was kind of interesting to watch. She had shared her observations with Jennifer who promptly assured her that it would wear off after a while, "kind of like those fake tattoos we stick on."

"How do you know so much?" quizzed Sarah.

"Do you see my parents acting like that?" retorted Jennifer confidently.

"No."

"Well, what more proof do you need?"

And so it was settled.

But despite the newlywed's frequent, *stop everything, I need a kiss break*, they managed to fill the carport with a wide assortment of garage sale merchandise. Piles of out-grown clothes, stacks of dog-eared paperbacks, dusty-covered hardbacks and forgotten toys and games were displayed with the hopes of a second chance in a new home. Boxes of mismatched dish sets, stained but still useful pots and pans, rusty tools requiring a facelift of elbow grease and oil, over-played CD's, DVD's and "like-new" exercise equipment lined the driveway, so customers could plow through the rubble with ease. Every inch of the borrowed picnic and card tables were crammed full with odd knick-knacks, unwanted decorations, unfinished craft projects, never-used time-saving appliances and crazy kitchen gadgets, all priced ridiculously low for quick haggle-free sales.

"And to think I prided myself on NOT being a pack-rat!" exclaimed Mrs. Conner, surveying the overcrowded carport.

"Funny how a move transforms *cherished possessions* into a pile of junk!" observed David, scratching his head in bewilderment.

"Just another one of life's unsolved mysteries," remarked Sarah nonchalantly.

"Good one, Sarah!" chuckled David.

"What will we do if no one buys anything?" asked Allison for the hundredth time.

"Would you quit worrying?" admonished Sarah. "And stop rearranging everything!"

"Whatever we don't sell is going straight to Goodwill!" announced Mrs. Conner with the authority of a Drill Sergeant.

At seven-thirty sharp, the first serious shoppers arrived driving a beat-up green station wagon that was already laden with early-bird specials. An older couple with identical protruding stomachs and frizzy gray mops, swiftly scrutinized the merchandise, picking up, examining, and setting down objects with curt nods and stony business-like expressions. A noisy dented pick-up truck sputtered to a squeaky halt behind the green wagon with a family of five (and one on the way) tumbled out of the cab, looking as if no one in this raggedy brood had ever used a comb. Allison quickly positioned herself to stand guard over her carefully arranged toy display, requiring the three curious, grimy faced youngsters to ask permission before handling anything of hers.

Spurred on by this encroaching competition, the older couple stopped their inspecting and suddenly began buying, much to Sarah's delight. As cashier, she was in charge of adding totals and making change while her mother assisted the customers with product information and wrapping breakable items before bagging them. Meanwhile, David was tidying up the house for the Realtor who had a ten o'clock showing to prospective buyers.

Soon, the neighbors meandered over, sipping steaming cups of coffee from *Best Mom* or *Is it Friday, Yet?* mugs. But they weren't serious buyers- they mostly came to chat and after thumbing through a stack of books or a pile of children's clothes, they trickled away with some small token trinket. Jennifer and Mike came over after watching their favorite cartoons with the express purpose of being allowed to "spend only five dollars." Sarah secretly notified Jennifer of her *best friend* sale causing Jennifer to agonize over the array of choices before her.

"I can't believe you're selling Crazy Cat," cried Jennifer, horrified at Sarah's lack of loyalty to a stuffed animal.

"She's a steal for two dollars," enticed Sarah, who actually hated the multi-colored feline with its goofy green stone eyes and stiff wiry whiskers. She had only kept it this long because her Aunt Flo had given it to her, and she didn't want to hurt her feelings. Where on earth Aunt Flo had bought this ugly creature had been a source of bewilderment, but Sarah never asked for fear of getting a matching dog. It certainly wasn't in any of the toy stores she shopped in. Thankfully, Aunt Flo was out-of-town this particular weekend, which proved to be, thought Sarah, chuckling to herself, the "purr-fect" opportunity to rid herself of the hideous monster.

"Gee, it's practically brand new," said Jennifer, admiring the tempting bargain. "I'll take it!" she succumbed gleefully, handing over two crumpled dollar bills.

"That's because I had to keep it in my closet, so Allison wouldn't get nightmares, uh, I mean, so she wouldn't sleep with it at night and crush it."

"I'm not the one who got nightmares," answered Allison abruptly, as Sarah quickly changed the subject.

"See anything you like, Mike?" she asked, as Mike feverishly picked through the meager remains of what the tow-headed kids had not carted away. While their parents scanned the *garage sale* ads in the newspaper, the kids piled their treasures on top of the accumulated clutter in the back of the pick-up. They drove slowly away, the old truck smoking and coughing all the way down the street, as Allison counted and recounted her haul.

At this point, Mike was starting to show signs of desperation and disappointment wasn't far behind. His contorted face couldn't decide whether to get mad and pout or to whine and cry.

"Here, Mike. How about my old water pistol?" suggested Sarah.

"That's only twenty-five cents." He grimaced as he accepted the gun.

"Here's a sand pail and some shovels," offered Jennifer.

"That still leaves me with three dollars," he moaned.

"Here's an alligator raft to take to the beach," said Mrs. Conner, pulling the deflated raft out of the laundry room.

"Yippee!" shouted Mike, now a satisfied customer.

"But, Mom," protested Sarah. "That's my favorite raft."

"I know, but we won't have much use for it in Kentucky," reasoned her mother.

"I was going to leave it at Grandma's for when we come to visit."

"We'll get a new one when we need it," said her mother with a wave of her hand.

Sarah couldn't argue with that. "Okay, Mike. Looks like you're all ready for the beach now."

"This will be great in our new pool!" said Mike between breaths, as the plastic alligator slowly grew to life.

"What new pool?" asked Sarah.

"The one we're building this summer. Didn't Jennifer tell you?"

"No," said Sarah eyeing Jennifer suspiciously.

"I sorta didn't want to tell you – with you moving and all," she said sheepishly.

"I don't believe it!" Sarah slapped her forehead in exasperation. "Here we are leaving right as you guys are getting a pool!"

By two o'clock, the well-stocked carport and driveway had dwindled down to a few slim pickings. David had joined them, bringing out lunch, so as not to "dirty up my clean kitchen" for the next Realtor appointment at three o'clock. "Shall we pack up these pitiful remains and call it a day?" he suggested.

"Yes, I'm tired of persnickety customers," groaned Mrs. Conner, lounging in a patio chair.

"How much money did we make?" asked Allison. "Enough to go out to eat, I hope."

Sarah, who had been keeping a running tally, totaled the final sale, then announced, "One hundred twenty-five dollars and fifty cents!"

"Not bad for a few hours work," remarked David.

"Can we go out to eat?" asked Allison anxiously.

"Yes, I guess we can afford it, squirt. Honestly, I don't know how you eat so much and stay so small," remarked Mrs. Conner.

"I have a good idea," blurted out Sarah. "Since the realtor is showing the house this afternoon, let's go to the beach and eat out there.

"Yeah!" agreed Allison.

"We can drop this stuff off on our way out," said David

All eyes were on Mrs. Conner, the final judge in such matters.

Ungluing herself from her comfortable recliner, she stretched, yawned, then said, "Don't forget the camera. This will be our last chance to see a beach sunset for a while."

Hearing that, Sarah's high spirits deflated like a leaky tire. She was excited about moving, but she hated to be reminded of the beautiful gulf beaches she'd practically grown up on. As if Mother Nature knew of their impending departure, the sunset that night was made to order. From behind the mounds of cotton candy clouds, the distant sky glowed a peachy orange flame. To Sarah, it looked as if a great fire was burning off in the distance, a beautiful, glowing fire, not a roaring destructive one. As the sun melted onto the ocean's surface, the intense flames deepened, adding a purple hue to the blending palette of colors. Breaks in the bumpy clouds revealed shadowy gray passages that seemed to beckon guardian angels to heaven's door for a relaxing meal after a hectic day's work.

Sarah couldn't stay sad for long. The beach cast its usual spell on her and she quickly found herself a captivated prisoner of its magic. *It's not as if I'll never see my beach again. It will be here waiting for me,* she told herself. And with that comforting thought, she sat on the beach wall with the other silent spectators, all lost in their final reflections of the day, hoping this celestial show would become an indelible imprint on her brain.

One thing about the sun – it says its goodnights promptly and never begs for another story, a last-minute drink of water or a final trip to the bathroom. But once the light is off and the room is black, a fading nightlight lingers, casting a faint pink glow on the ceiling above, so the evening stars can find their way in the dark.

*   *   *

During Sarah's short life, she had traveled on yawning stretches of highways, dusty unpaved country lanes and slick well-oiled avenues. Moving, as she quickly discovered, was definitely the traffic jam of life. Like over-heated cars with bubbling radiators and noxious-fuming trucks stuck in rush hour grid-lock, so were the feelings and experiences of moving – jammed together for a brief, nerve-wracking block of time.

For one thing, moving was hard. Having to say good-bye to friends, classmates and a favorite teacher, and knowing that life would go on without you is a difficult pill to swallow. Trying to imagine a new life in a new state was a pill so large, it couldn't be swallowed! And rather than choking, it was easier just to spit it out and not think about it.

For another, moving was hectic. There was always something that needed to be done *right now* or something that *should have been settled yesterday* and don't forget the ever-popular, *be sure to take care of that first thing tomorrow morning!* Assorted shapes and sizes of *To Do* lists lay scattered around the house like litter after the state fair has left town. And the poor phone! It never got to sleep before midnight and was usually the first one up!

Last, but not least, moving was hilarious, sort of. Living out of a suitcase with mismatched socks, not enough clean underwear and forgotten deodorant while traveling with a car-sick cat who meowed like a non-stop merry-go-round and a forty-pound dog that hogged the front seat, panting hot, smelly dog-breath in your face and licking your hamburger – well, you had to laugh, otherwise, you'd go insane!

"M" Day arrived at an alarming rate of speed. As Sarah chewed the last of her cherry Pop-Tart, a giant shoe-box shaped truck rumbled up the street, its empty insides clattering and banging like some hungry monster demanding to be fed. It stopped in front the house, blocking everyone's view and giving Sarah that trapped nowhere to turn feeling. Two uniformed men jumped down from the steep cab and swung open the wide side-doors, revealing the un-fed belly of the van. Like a pull-toy on a string, a mini-van chugged up behind and out of it hopped two more men and three women. Dressed in bright yellow T-shirts with the words, *We move every family as if it were our own!* and black slacks. Sarah overheard David as he leaned over and smirked in the ear of her mother, "I hope they aren't on bad terms with their families!"

"Yeah," giggled her mother. "They might be anxious to get rid of us!"

Sarah couldn't help snickering at their private joke, as the packers descended upon the house like a hoard of worker bees that couldn't wait to get back to their queen. The oldest of the three women invaded the kitchen with heaps of packing paper and stacks of thick cardboard dish-packs. The other women stationed themselves in Sarah and Allison's bedrooms, while the men tackled the living and dining room.

"You girls have a terrific last day of school," said Mrs. Conner, ushering them hastily out the door.

"But I didn't brush my teeth," protested Allison.

The door slammed quickly behind them.

"I feel like I've just been kicked out of my own house," groused Sarah to Allison, who wasn't listening.

"We're lucky because we get out of school a week early!" she replied, as if that made the whole move worthwhile.

"Big deal," grumbled Sarah, who was having serious second thoughts about this whole thing.

They spent the night with Grandma, who decided to throw a traditional Thanksgiving dinner.

"Mom, you didn't have to go to all this trouble," said Mrs. Conner.

"I wanted to do it. It kept my mind occupied these past few days; otherwise I'd be a worthless lump of wet tears by now." She smiled sadly.

"Why don't you spend Thanksgiving with us in Kentucky this year?" invited David.

"Thank-you, David but I don't tolerate cold weather very well. Living in Florida for so many years has made my blood thin. If it goes below seventy degrees, I need a heavy sweater!"

"We'll turn the heat up on high, Grandma," offered Allison hopefully.

"I know you would, Dear, but I have an old friend in Sarasota who's been after me for ages to come spend a few weeks with her. She's expecting me in October and I wouldn't want to disappoint her," explained Grandma gently.

"What about Christmas, then?" asked Sarah, who was starting to wonder if she'd ever see her grandmother again.

"I was hoping you'd come stay with me over the holidays," she hinted. "You might be ready for a little warm weather by then!"

"It's a deal!" agreed David.

Early the next morning, several tearful good-byes were said before they drove by the house for a final farewell and to make sure they hadn't left anything behind. Sarah walked through the vacant house, her footsteps echoing an eerie hollow sound she now suddenly felt in her heart. This house and neighborhood had been her entire world for eleven years. She already missed her grandma and Jennifer and all the special times they had shared. The empty house looked lonely and sad. Her bedroom that had been completely intact yesterday, looked as if a hurricane had blown through, taking all her possessions with it. The cold bare walls and undressed windows made her shiver and the exposed terrazzo floor was as slick and shiny as an ice-skating rink. She sighed dismally. Someone else would have to come in and make this house a home again.

Being a school day and a work day, the neighborhood was as quiet as a church on Monday morning. The two remaining homemakers on the street were probably at their aerobics classes, so there was no one to stand by and wave, as Grandma had done, clutching her tear-stained hanky.

Mrs. Conner choked back a few involuntary tears.

"Are you all right?" asked David, squeezing her hand.

"Yes," she nodded. "We said our good-byes yesterday. It's really much easier this way."

Sarah crawled into the backseat. She had said her good-byes to Jennifer over the phone last night.

"Will you call me?" asked Jennifer, who loved to talk, even more than texting.

"As soon as I have something interesting to tell," promised Sarah.

"And you won't forget to send me a picture of your horse – when you get it, that is."

"I'll send you so many pictures, you'll get sick of them!" joked Sarah. "Hey, maybe you can visit me next summer and we can ride double."

"As long as he's gentle," cautioned Jennifer.

"Don't worry, he'll be perfect!" assured Sarah confidently.

And then they said, *see ya later*, like it was any other normal call.

*   *   *

After two boring days of monotonous interstates and exits, smelly gas stations, an endless array of junk food and one cheap motel without a pool, Sarah was startled out of one of the dozen or so cat-naps she had lapsed into. "Huh? What'd you say David?"

"I said we're approaching horse country now."

"Really? You mean we're actually getting close?" She sat up, wiped the drool that was collecting in the corner of her mouth and peered out the window like a tourist on a bus trip.

At first, her sleepy eyes wouldn't focus, and all she saw was a blue-green blur rushing by that sort of resembled the ocean she'd left behind. Moving tracks of white fences raced past her like a white locomotive. Finally, the fences and fields came into focus, leaving Sarah breathless. Sprawling before her, in every direction, were the rolling fields of Kentucky, casting their famous blue-green tinge like waves on a sunny breezy day. But where were the horses? Surely, there had to be a herd of mares and foals grazing on this glorious spring day. Straining her eyes, she scanned the landscape at each new bend in the two-lane road that twisted and turned like a lazy snake, giving Sarah that sinking, then churning feeling in the pit of her stomach – the kind you get right before you . . .

"Gross!! Get away from me!" shrieked Allison. "Mom, Sarah's throwing up!"

"David, pull over," cried Mrs. Conner.

"Can't . There's not enough shoulder room between the road and the ditch."

"Yuk! It stinks," wailed Allison, holding her nose.

"Roll the window down, for heaven's sake," admonished Mrs. Conner.

"Where'd it land? Not on the seat, I hope," David wondered aloud.

"Most of it managed to hit the floor," said Mrs. Conner, craning her neck around to observe the damage. "Sarah, did your lunch disagree with you? I hope you didn't get food poisoning at that last stop. Those burgers didn't taste very fresh to me, and they looked a little undercooked. Allison, how do you feel?" she said, reaching over to feel Allison's forehead.

"I was fine until she puked all over the place."

"I thought you said it landed on the floor," said David anxiously.

Sarah looked up weakly and sputtered. "I think I got carsick."

"That's it!" exclaimed David. "It's these corkscrew roads. From now on, she'll have to ride these country roads in the front seat."

"We'll stop as soon as we can, honey. We can't risk getting side-swiped on these blind curves. How do you feel now?" asked her mother.

"Awful. My mouth tastes terrible."

"Here, sip some soda. It'll help settle your stomach."

With nowhere to put her feet, Sarah sat cross-legged for the next ten miles, Instead of being surrounded by beautiful thoroughbreds as she'd hoped, she found herself staring at sprayed vomit in front of, below and beside her. Allison jammed herself as close to her door as she could, and leaned her head out the window like a dog on a joy ride.

"Allison, stop leaning against the door. The last thing I need is for you to fall out," said Mrs. Conner, exasperated.

"It's locked," protested Allison.

"I don't care. Do as I say and don't argue with me."

Reluctantly, Allison relinquished an inch. "That's as far as I'm going!"

Sarah couldn't really blame Allison. It was pretty gross being trapped with your own vomit, much less someone else's. At last, they came to a fork in the road with an old-timey gas station and general store tucked snugly between the V-shaped split. David pulled into the gravel parking lot whereupon Allison practically leaped out of the still-moving car. Besides feeling squeamish and stinky, Sarah wished she could crawl underneath a rock and hide. How embarrassing to throw-up in front of everyone and in David's new car, of all places. *He's probably wishing he'd never gone through with this marriage, now.*

"Most of it's on the floor mat," shouted her mother, for all the world to hear, as she started to hose it down.

I hope he's not too mad at me. He'll probably make me carry a barf bag every time I ride in his car, she thought ruefully, trudging slowly behind as he and Allison entered the store.

"Excuse me," said David politely to a gray-haired woman sitting behind the counter, "do you have a ladies restroom?"

"My sister threw up in the car," announced Allison dramatically.

"You don't have to blab to everybody, big mouth!" snapped Sarah, under her breath.

"In the back to your right," answered the woman, without looking up from her magazine.

David put his arm across Sarah's shoulders and walked her to the back of the store.

"I'm sorry, David. I didn't mean to mess up your car," she stammered.

"It's okay. After all, it's not as if you threw up on purpose."

"That's for sure," she groaned in agreement.

"Just between you and me, I have a confession to make," he whispered loudly.

"What is it?" asked Sarah, who loved secrets.

"When I was about your age, I lived near the mountains in Tennessee and those back roads are like a pile of spaghetti on your plate. I used to get so carsick, my parents made me ride in the back of our pickup truck with our beagle, Mack!"

"Oh, David, that couldn't be true. You're just saying that to make me feel better."

"Wait till we get my old photo albums unpacked. You'll see. Actually, it was a pretty good system. Afterwards, Dad would just hose ole' Bessie out. And away goes trouble down the drain!" sang David.

"You're just teasing me," she blushed.

"No, for real. Scout's honor. Poor Dad," sighed David. "He never could sell that truck. Too many stains and of course, that lingering aroma didn't help any!"

"David, stop!" she laughed, holding her aching side. Catching her breath, she asked, "Is this going to happen every time we ride down this road?"

"No you'll probably outgrow it eventually, but until then, we'll take the necessary precautions!"

"What are those?"

"Well, since we don't have a truck, we'll just strap you to the roof of the car,' he said, tousling her hair.

Sarah couldn't stop grinning as she cleaned herself up. Thank goodness, David was so understanding. Jennifer's dad would have pitched a fit for weeks.

"Only five more miles to Wilmore," David winked to Sarah who had traded places with her mother.

Between the bubble gum and breath mints, her mouth tasted better and the lingering aroma from the back seat was quickly becoming a thing of the past as blasts of fresh air absorbed the odor and carried it out the window never to be smelled again.

At last, the sight of bronze-colored mares cantering effortlessly alongside the fence came into view. Best of all, were the frolicking foals prancing and bucking in the warm glow of the afternoon sun.

"Looks like a welcoming committee," commented Mrs. Conner.

"It won't be long now. We're almost home."

Chapter Four

Wilmore

It didn't take a brain surgeon to figure out why Sarah got so carsick. It was especially obvious when trying to pedal a one-geared purple bike decorated with a glittery silver banana seat and bright rainbow streamers – all show and now totally useless and out-of-place along the hilly, winding, rural roads. Sarah found herself cringing in embarrassment every time a sleek ten-speed racer zoomed by, which was often, as college students and professors glided effortlessly to class. It was odd how one could adore a bike in a particular setting and despise it in another. Along the flat streets of suburban Tampa, she had one of the most popular bikes in the neighborhood – one that everybody asked to ride. *No chance of that here*, she thought, as she huffed and puffed her way up a steep steady incline.

"I must look like a circus clown," she grunted between breaths, then grinned as she envisioned herself. *All I need is a dancing white poodle with pink toenails and a tutu to complete the picture.* Suddenly a new dilemma presented itself. Should she ask for a new bike first or a horse? Maybe she could ask for the horse as an early birthday present from her parents since she would be turning 12 in September and money for the bike from her grandmother. "That should work," she mused, as her mind worked out the details.

Spotting a pair of dullish brown ponies dozing under a large shady oak, their long tangled tails swishing away pesky horseflies, her mind quickly shifted gears to the horse she dreamed of owning. Her well-meaning grandmother had suggested a plump plodding pony- how boring! No, Sarah already had ideas of her own. For weeks before the move, she had poured over her vast collection of horse magazines and had scoured the internet and library for every *Your First Horse* book she could find. After much thoughtful deliberation and a few agonizing moments, she had finally settled on the beautifully versatile Morgan as her first choice or the muscular but lightning fast Quarter Horse as an ideal second choice. Both breeds were rather expensive, especially the Morgan, but it seemed only logical to buy a well bred horse she would never outgrow or tire of.

If only her father could help select her dream horse then life would truly be perfect. Gazing at the vast open sky, a memory as wispy as the thin clouds overhead wafted faintly across her mind. It was a far-away memory, and she could barely make it out, but like a blurry watercolor, there was her father playing "horsey back ride" with her. *I must have been only two or three, but I never remembered this before.* "Oh, Dad, I wish you were here," she cried out, her heart suddenly aching the way it had for months after the funeral.

Tears welled up, obscuring her vision. Stopping her bike, she laid it by the side of the road and hiked through the open pasture to a half-rotten log hidden in the tall grass. Sitting down, she thought back to when her father had died. She had not only been grief-stricken, but terribly confused. She, along with many others, had fervently prayed for her father's life to be spared, but it seemed God had turned a deaf ear towards everyone during those terrifying hours. Later, after the funeral, she asked her mother why God hadn't answered her prayer. As difficult as it was, her mother tried to explain, but it didn't make much sense at the time. She knew other kids whose parents had divorced, but not any who had a parent die. It was so unfair. Why her father when there were so many dead beat dads who didn't care a thing about their kids? Why couldn't it have been someone like that? Thinking back, now that she was older, the explanation made a little more sense, but it was still no easier to accept.

"Sarah, God never promised us perfect lives free from sorrow or pain. But He did promise to be with us through good times and bad."

"Don't you miss Daddy?" Sarah sniffed back tears.

"Of course I do, sweetheart. Every moment of every day. But knowing Daddy's in heaven gives me great comfort, and one day, we'll all be together again."

After that, the conversation was as fuzzy as a windowpane splashed with heavy raindrops. Burying her head in her lap, Sarah wept once more for people and places that once were, but would never be again. Lifting her head, she wiped her eyes with her shirt sleeve then looked heavenward. "I love you, Dad," she whispered. "I miss you so much, but please tell God thank-you for sending David to be with us." She sat quietly for a few minutes watching everything but seeing nothing. Heaving a weary sigh, she returned to her bike, looked up at the sky, and was suddenly amazed to see a reassuring bright rainbow telling her heart that her Dad wasn't so very far away.

Mounting her bike with a new fervor, she faced a rising incline and decided to tackle the steep rise. *Who needs a ten speed anyway? There's only one way to enjoy the ride down!* With the fortitude of an Olympic athlete, she half rode and half pushed her purple one-speed up and up and, like a roller coaster cresting before its wild rushing descent, she paused a moment to catch her breath when she reached the top. "This must be the steepest hill in town," she panted, wiping away the beads of sweat from her brow and upper lip. Also the best view, she thought, admiring the sections of fields, crops, and woods that spread across the landscape like a giant patchwork quilt, "Mom can't say there's no place to keep a horse around here!" she shouted, as she joyously coasted down the hill, the summer breeze cooling her brow and drying her sweaty moustache. At the bottom, she looked up and exclaimed, "Wow! What a great hill for sledding!"

Having only seen snow on television and in the movies, she couldn't wait for winter.

In Sarah's mind, a list was quickly forming - *Let's see, besides sledding, there's snowmen and snow forts to build, snowball fights, snow angels and snow ice cream and maybe one day a sleigh ride pulled by my very own handsome Morgan!*

Allison was sitting on the front steps when she rode up the driveway. "Don't park it yet. Mom wants you to go to the store."

"Not again. I just went this morning," moaned Sarah, who was ready to eat. "Hey, why don't you ever go?"

"Don't have a big enough basket on my bike," reminded Allison. "And Mom doesn't think I'm old enough yet."

"Oh, yeah, I forgot," Sarah grinned sheepishly.

Pedaling to the store, her petulant mood disappeared as quickly as it had arrived. She really didn't mind riding the half mile to the quaint town square. But between Fitch's Family Grocery and Harold's Hardware Heaven (Harold preached on Sundays and liked to remind his customers of their need for a firm foundation both in this world and the one to come), It seemed as if Sarah spent at least an hour a day running errands. She was already well acquainted with the cashiers and the bag boy, who wasn't a boy at all, but old Mr. Fitch, who proudly and precisely bagged groceries six days a week "to keep an eye on my boys who run the place now!" Sarah liked Mr. Fitch instantly. He was short and stooped over, and he wore red suspenders and a black bow tie attached to a crisp white shirt every day. He shuffled his feet and muttered a lot to himself, but he knew every little thing going on in his store. "See this white fuzz?" he said, pointing to the wispy white ring of hair circling his shiny bald head.

Sarah nodded.

"That's my halo," he confided with a wink. "Having that halo is just like having eyes in the back of your head. Comes with age and wisdom," he declared proudly.

"My mom doesn't have a halo, and she has eyes in the back of her head," remarked Sarah skeptically.

"Ah, yes it's true; mothers seem to come equipped that way. But as a general rule, fathers aren't endowed with such gifts until they have lost most of their hair!" Mr. Fitch chuckled good- naturedly.

One thing about Fitch's Family Grocery, it certainly lived up to its name. Every employee bore the Fitch name on their nametag. There were "the boys," Freddie and Frankie Fitch, who "now ran the place," but had actually been managing things for nearly twenty years, and spinster nieces Floetta and Florence, who worked as cashiers and loved to dress exactly alike even though they were five years apart in age. Uncle Foster and Aunt Fannie Fitch cut and packaged the meat and poultry- they also butchered hogs and steer for the local farmers and dressed deer and turkeys during hunting season, while cousin Fletcher and his boy, Felix, handled the produce. Mr. Fitch's wife, Fiona, was Sarah's favorite. She worked in the bakery/deli and always gave Sarah "an ample sample" from the warmest tray of fresh baked cookies or brownies.

"There was one exception to this name game and that was Freddie's wife, Phoebe, the bookkeeper. In order to avoid calling attention to this breach of tradition, they had secretly eloped right after their high school graduation.

"But to show our good intentions, we named our daughters Francine and Frieda," laughed Phoebe, who loved to tell newcomers how she finagled her way into the Fitch family.

"Well, it still sounds like an F and that's what counts!" reminded Mr. Fitch, who always got the last word.

Despite her entertaining surroundings, Sarah was anxious to settle the gnawing restlessness eating away at her. She had been waiting all her life for a horse and now that they had lived in Wilmore for nearly two weeks, she thought she'd go insane if she had to wait much longer. But the few times she'd attempted the subject, her mother was either too tired or not feeling well enough to discuss it. Had she forgotten her promise? No, her mother wasn't like that. Maybe she had changed her mind. Sarah shuddered at the thought and silently prayed it wasn't so? Going to David wouldn't help any. She knew he'd just say "You'll have to talk to your mother about that."

So for now, Sarah was forced to bide her time and bite her tongue. Catching her mother at the right mood was crucial – it could mean the difference between a beautiful Morgan or a pokey little pony that plodded along at a snail's pace. Sarah understood her mother was busy settling in but how much more work could there be? The spacious old house seemed to be in good order. All the furniture was in place and most of the boxes had been emptied and taken to the recycling center. Only the guest bedroom downstairs remained empty with her mother murmuring something about leaving it for the time being- she'd tend to later. She probably wants to fix it up nice for Grandma, reasoned Sarah, who liked the aged house and knew her grandmother would too, even though it was very different from their ranch style house in Florida.

To be sure, there were some eyesores, such as the hideous floral wallpaper in the dining room that looked as if it came right out of someone's nightmare and the rusty discolored bathtub but even with its peeling white paint and missing green shutters, the old house had the warmth and charm of an elderly, yet genteel southern belle, wearing patched gloves and thin tattered petticoats.

She was quite taken with her attic bedroom, which resembled a cozy cave like den, with its low slanting ceiling and one small screenless window overlooking the driveway below. "This window will be great for spying," she told Allison that afternoon. "All we need is a pair of binoculars."

"David has a pair in his study," remarked Allison casually. "Maybe he'll let us borrow them sometime."

"Are you sure?"

"Yes, because I helped him unpack. He uses them for bird watching."

"Bird watching! How dull!" Sarah yawned dramatically. "Spying on people is a lot more interesting!" she said, scanning the quiet neighborhood below. Then, turning to Allison, she said, "Well? What are you waiting for? Go get them."

"Don't you think we should ask him first?"

"He won't be home for a couple more hours. Anyway, I just want to use them for a few minutes. Ask Mom, if you're so worried."

"She's taking a nap."

"Again? That's all she ever does, lately."

"David said the move's been hard on her."

"Didn't seem that hard to me," mused Sarah. "She'd be upset if we woke her up just for this."

"Let's just wait till David gets home. Then we can use them for as long as we want," reasoned Allison.

"I only want to use them for a few minutes! Go on, Allison, go get them!"

"No way. Mom told us not to go in David's study unless he was in there."

"What are binoculars doing in an office anyway? That's a stupid place. Where are they? I'll get them myself, you big baby."

"Better not," warned Allison.

"Allison, you are such a miss priss, sometimes. If David was here, I'd ask him and he'd say yes. It's as simple as that. Now where are they?" she demanded

"In the bottom drawer of his file cabinet," confessed Allison reluctantly.

Tiptoeing down the narrow attic stairs, Sarah grimaced at every squeak as she stole across the wooden floors into David's office. The drawer slid open with ease and leaving it open, she cautiously scurried back upstairs like a cat with her prey. The last thing she wanted to do was wake her mother and put her in a bad mood. Maybe this evening would be THE evening to ask!

"Wow! I can almost see to the edge of town with these things! They must really be powerful."

"Let me see, let me see!" begged Allison.

"I shouldn't give you a turn, chicken little."

"Please…"

"Okay, but be careful."

"Sarah, there's a pony in someone's front yard!" squealed Allison.

"Yeah, right. Here, let me see. It's probably just a big dog."

"No, it's a black pony eating grass," insisted Allison.

"Hey, you're right! And there's a man trying to catch him, I think. Come on, maybe we can help him."

"We're not supposed to talk to strangers!" hissed Allison sharply.

"That was when we lived in a big city," Sarah rationalized. "Are you going with me or not?"

"No, I'm staying here," answered Allison firmly.

Leaving the binoculars on her bed, Sarah hurried downstairs quickly and quietly as she could. The street was only two blocks away and she reached it in record-breaking speed. Spotting the grazing pony, she parked her bike behind a shrub and slowly approached as a grandfatherly looking farmer dressed in faded blue overalls and a pale blue work shirt, tried to sweetly cajole the loose pony to him.

"Come on, Stormy. Come to Virgil like a good boy," he cooed softly. "Lookee here, I got a nice juicy apple for ya. And not a single worm in it." But as Virgil slowly inched forward, the pony took an equal number of steps farther away and continued his grazing. Exasperated, Virgil took off his Kentucky Wildcats cap, revealing a dazzling white head of hair. With a matching beard, thought Sarah, he could be Santa Claus' twin brother. Except for his belly. That would need fattening up or a pillow to fill out the suit. Using his gnarled, weathered fingers as a comb, he ran his hands through his thick flowing locks, his patient tone turning to annoyance. "Durn it, Stormy! The grass here ain't any better than the grass in yer pasture. I'm getting too old for this foolishness."

Sarah watched intently as Virgil and Stormy edged their way into the backyard. Struck with an idea, she crossed the street, so as not to spook Stormy, walked past the next house and crossed back. Then she cut across the neighboring backyard with the hope of catching the runaway herself. Hiding behind a leafy wild rosebush, she waited until Stormy was so close, she could almost reach out and grab his halter. Like a blooming flower, she slowly revealed herself, gently calling his name.

Caught by surprise, Stormy's curiosity overtook him and leaning towards her, he sniffed her out stretched palm. Silently chiding herself for not grabbing a carrot out of the crisper, she had to rely on scratching his whiskery chin, then working her way up to the soft downy fur behind his ears. Distracted by this pleasure, Sarah casually took hold of his green halter while Virgil slipped up beside her and snapped the lead rope in place.

Heaving a sigh of relief, he tipped his cap and thanked Sarah profusely.

"How did he get loose?" she asked, admiring the large spunky pony.

"He kin find a weak spot in any fence. And no matter how often I fix it, he finds another way out. He's even been known to open a gate or two!" Virgil chuckled as he fondly rubbed Stormy's broad back. "He's jest too clever for his own good – a regular escape artist, that's what he is!"

"He's very pretty and big, too, for a pony. What breed is he?"

"Oh, he's what ya call a grade horse. You know, a mixture of this and that, like a mutt. But he turned out right well formed. A few more inches and he'd be an official horse." Turning to Stormy, he exclaimed, "Stormy! Where are our manners? We haven't been properly introduced. All this excitement done made me forget myself. I'm Virgil Reed and this here's Stormy."

"I'm Sarah Taylor," said Sarah awkwardly. She wasn't very good at introductions.

"Well, I'm pleased to make yer acquaintance, Miss Sarah. But I don't recollect your face."

"We just moved here from Florida. My stepdad's a new professor at the college."

"Welcome to Wilmore. How do ya like it so far?"

"I like it a lot, but I'll really love it when I get my own horse."

"So, yer planning on gettin' a horse – well, this is horse country, that's fer sure."

"Do you have a horse farm?" she asked, expectantly.

"No, missy, I'm afraid not," he answered with an amused smile. "I got my hands full with Stormy here and a few other critters that don't give me so much grief!"

"But you do have a farm, don't you?" she persisted.

"Sure do. I have a few acres right past the edge of the town. Between my critters and my crops, I stay busy enough."

"Too busy to be out here chasing a runaway, I bet!" teased Sarah, good-naturedly.

"You got that right, missy!" laughed Virgil. "Which reminds me, I better start headin' back afore my sister, Virginia starts fretting about my whereabouts!" Sliding onto Stormy's wide back, he added, "If ya need a place to board that new horse of yers, jest gimme a call. I got plenty of room. Hmmm, maybe we could work out somethin'. Me an' Ginny could always use a little extra help around the place. You could start with exercising this ornery fella."

"Gee, thanks Mr. Reed. That sounds great!" exclaimed Sarah in near disbelief.

"Speak to yer folks about it. My number's in the book. And for heaven's sake, call me Virgil. I don't answer to Mr. Reed!" he said with a cheery wink.

Sarah watched, dumbfounded, as Virgil and Stormy, now surprisingly obedient, trotted briskly down the sidewalk.

Had she heard right? Had he practically said she could board her horse for free in exchange for helping out?

"Yes!" she shouted, jumping on her bike. The sooner this was settled, the better!

She felt as if she were living in a dream. The question of where to keep a horse had been instantly solved! *And I didn't even pray about this yet.* Now she was glad she hadn't asked for a horse earlier. Her mother couldn't say no now, not for any reason.

Dropping her bike in the front yard, she skipped up the front steps where the dream suddenly curdled like sour milk on a hot day. The thrilling plans forming in her mind jammed in reverse and lodged in her throat when she saw the three of them sitting on the porch swing- Allison, her eyes red and nose sniffing, David, with a pair of shattered binoculars in his lap and her mother, lips pursed and face tense with anger.

"Where have you been?" Mrs. Conner asked tersely.

"Didn't Allison tell you?" her voice cracked.

"Since when is it Allison's responsibility to keep track of you?" Without letting Sarah answer, she continued. "First, you take something without permission, then you run off on some wild goose chase with a stranger, without permission, and then you don't even have the common sense to put these binoculars back!"

Sarah gulped. "Sorry."

"Would you please explain your actions?"

"I just wanted to borrow them for a few minutes, and we saw this old man trying to catch his pony. I didn't think David would mind. Then I left them on my bed. I was going to return when I got back," she mumbled, her eyes never leaving the floor.

"I told you we had to ask David, first!" blurted out Allison. "Now I'm being punished because of you!" she wailed.

"Well, you broke them!" shot back Sarah. "Why didn't you just leave 'em alone and none of this would've happened! You probably threw them out the window just so I'd get in trouble!"

"No, I did not! I was trying to see you and the pony, and they slipped and fell!"

"Sarah, none of this would have happened, if you had shown any respect for my belongings and my request," reminded David firmly.

Sarah was silent. She was not accustomed to David being angry with her. It was bound to happen eventually, she thought, but why now?

"You ought to be thankful your sister didn't fall out with them!" snapped Mrs. Conner.

"I'll put a screen up this evening," said David.

Taking a big breath, Mrs. Conner went on. "We have several problems to deal with. First of all, you never leave this house without telling me or David where you're going."

"But you were sleeping!" interrupted Sarah.

"Then leave a note on the kitchen table or text me- you know all this, Sarah. The rules haven't changed. And now you're going to have to pay David for the binoculars you broke."

"But I didn't break them." Now it was Sarah's turn to cry.

"You are the person responsible for them, and it's going to cost you $125.00 to replace them."

"A hundred and twenty-five dollars!" screeched Sarah. "How can I pay all that by myself? It'll take me the rest of my life. What about her? What's her punishment?"

"Her punishment is none of your concern," answered David.

"You can use some of your savings for a start. The rest you'll have to earn or work off," explained Mrs. Conner.

"But my savings is my horse money," protested Sarah. "You promised I could get a horse if we ever had a place to keep one, and I found a place today."

"Sarah, your behavior today shows me you are not mature enough to handle the responsibility of caring for a horse. And besides that, we don't have enough extra money to spend on a horse right now," said Mrs. Conner.

"You said when we moved here I could get a horse!" she shouted.

"Lower your voice, young lady. I said we'd seriously look into it."

"And we will, Sarah," David broke in gently. "We're not saying you can never get a horse. Just not right now."

"Well, when?" she cried.

"When you're a little older – in a year or two," said her mother.

"A year or two? I might as well not get one at all!" Now the floodgates were open and the tears were spilling down her cheeks in torrents. "I'm old enough. Lots of girls my age have horses."

"Sarah, our budget is stretched to the limit until the house in Florida is sold. We can't afford any extras right now."

"I thought you were going to get another nursing job, Mom," said Allison.

"No, I'm going to be staying home for a while."

"How come?" Sarah's throat hurt.

David and Amy looked at each other and smiled. "Your mother's going to have a baby!" he announced proudly.

"A baby? You gotta be kidding!" exclaimed Sarah, who thought she was going to die right there on the porch.

"You mean I'm not going to be the youngest anymore?" asked Allison eagerly.

"No, you'll be in the middle, sweetheart," said Mrs. Conner.

"Can I help with the baby?"

"Of course you can. I'll need a lot of help, from everybody."

"Yippee!"

Sarah didn't, couldn't, wouldn't hear anymore. Without a word, she marched upstairs, slammed her door and threw herself on her bed so mad she couldn't even cry.

Chapter Five

Unexpected News

Two hours later, Sarah was still fuming. How could they treat her this way? What if Allison hadn't broken the binoculars? What excuse would they make then for not allowing her to get a horse? That baby reason could only be stretched so far. And as for money, well, her grandmother would have paid for the horse and probably some of the expenses.

"Oh, God why is this happening to me?" Hearing no reply, she stared at the slanted ceiling above her. She felt like a yo-yo these past few months what with the marriage, the move and now the worst news of all – a baby on the way! Between indentured servitude to David and being drafted against her will as mother's little helper, the future had turned into a deep dark well with slimy green walls and no way of escape. A fleeting thought occurred to her that she might ask to live with her grandmother, but she quickly tossed that impossibility aside. They'd never agree to that. No, she'd have to think of something else. But Sarah's anger over *THE BETRAYAL* kept getting in the way. *First, they take away my horse and then they practically dump a baby in my lap!* Didn't they realize a baby affects everyone in a family?

(Especially the oldest). And they had only been a family for a few weeks! They had discussed their marriage and this move; why not a baby, for heaven's sake? Now their lives would have to revolve around *the baby!* Sarah sneered. She already resented its intrusion. And no matter what anyone said, it was always the oldest that got stuck with the "crappy" jobs. Well, they could forget it! There was no way she, Sarah Taylor, was changing a stinky poopy diaper!

Suddenly, she let out a stifled gasp as a horrible new thought struck her. What if her mother had twins or decided to have more kids after this one? She watched the unthinkable scene in horror – they'd be like Old Mother Hubbard with so many children, she didn't know what to do! But instead of amusement from her over active imagination, piercing jabs of betrayal stung her wounded heart.

A light knock at the door broke her trance. "Sarah, I brought you some dinner," said David, but she refused to answer.

"May I come in?"

"I'd rather not." Her words trembled with shame and embarrassment. How could she ever face him again?

"I understand. I'll leave your dinner out here. Try to eat something, okay?"

She listened to his footsteps descending the narrow attic stairs. "I guess he won't be putting in a screen, tonight," she grumbled to her stuffed animals.

Leaning out the infamous window, she wondered how many other kids had gotten into trouble because of this tempting overlook. Gazing upward, her turbulent mood was no match for the tranquil evening sky, where the waning sun was hidden behind a solitary gray cloud. "What am I going to do now, God?" she whispered more to herself than to God. Sighing she watched the lonely little cloud slowly reveal a dazzling rim of gold with filtered rays of hope penetrating its center. Caught in the cloud's mystical web, Sarah was startled when an idea popped into her muddled head – an idea so clear, so perfect, she almost shouted. Instead, she uttered a sincere prayer of thanks. She couldn't imagine why she hadn't thought of it earlier. Might have saved herself a little anguish. Maybe this was what her grandmother had meant when she'd say, "Every dark cloud has a silver lining, Sarah."

Her silver lining was Virgil, of course! He was the answer to her prayers. Hadn't he offered her a job? Maybe, instead of boarding a horse in exchange for chores, he could pay her. Maybe she could even get paid to ride Stormy! Sarah shook her head in amazement. Imagine being paid to ride!

Her burden somewhat lightened, she acknowledged her growling stomach and hungrily retrieved her dinner. As she ate, she realized this would also get her out of the house for most of the day, thus avoiding the dreaded pregnancy with all its daily reminders: morning sickness, swollen ankles and the ever popular craving spells that would increase with her mother's expanding belly! "Guess Allison better get a bigger basket," she giggled to herself. "Let her go get the giant jars of pickles and the gallons of ice cream!"

After Sarah finished her meal, she took her plate to the kitchen and quietly prepared for bed. From the living room, she heard the drone of the television and Allison munching on popcorn before she sealed herself off in the bathroom. The hot shower spray relaxed her tense body, allowing her to formulate her plan. She'd make a big announcement at breakfast – no, that wouldn't work. She had to sneak a call to Virgil, first. The announcement would have to wait until dinner. *They'll be so impressed they might change their minds and let me get a horse this summer!*

She slept late the next morning, and found a note when she came down for breakfast:

Sarah, I have a doctor's appt. this morning and a few errands to run, so we'll talk when I get back. Allison is with me. Please mow the lawn & clean both bathrooms. Love, Mom

Wolfing down her cereal and toast, she hurried outside to mow before it got too hot. When she finished the front, she went inside for a drink and decided to call Virgil. Although there was nearly a full page of Reeds listed, the number was easy to find since there was only one Virgil and Virginia Reed. Dialing the number, her optimism soured. What if no one was at home? Or what if Virginia answered? What would she say? How should she explain the predicament she was in?

"Hello?" a gruff, but friendly sounding voice answered.

"Uh, hello. Is this the Reed residence?" Sarah's voice was shaky. She wasn't used to talking to grownups, other than her grandmother, on the phone.

"Yes, what kin I do fer ya?"

"Uh, Virgil, this is Sarah Taylor. I helped you catch Stormy yesterday."

"Hello there, missy! Did ya speak with yer folks yet?"

"Well, not yet. You see, something's come up, and I was wondering if I could work for pay instead of for boarding a horse?"

"Hmmm. I'll have to think on that fer a spell. Most of my spare cash is tied up in my crops and cattle until fall. You'd have to get by on IOU's until my corn and soybeans are harvested. Are ya havin' to save up for this here horse of yers?"

"Well sort of." Sarah hesitated. She didn't want to lie to Virgil, but she didn't want him to think her irresponsible or careless. "My sister and I accidently broke our step-father's binoculars and…,"

"Say no more, missy. How much do ya need to earn?"

"Around a hundred dollars." Sarah gulped, hoping it wasn't too much.

"Them musta been some fancy spyglasses."

"Yes, sir, they were."

"Lemme speak with Ginny, and I'll give ya a call back this evening. Are yer folks agreeable to this?"

"Well, I haven't exactly had a chance to bring it up. I thought I should check with you first."

"Sensible thinkin'. I tell ya what. Call me back after ya've had a chance to speak with 'em, and then we'll work out the details."

Elated, Sarah did an extra good job on the bathrooms, and when Mrs. Conner and Allison returned, they found Sarah weeding the scraggly flower bed.

"Okay, 'fess up."

"What are you talking about, Mom?"

"You know what I'm talking about. Since when do you volunteer for a chore?"

"Well, there is something I need to ask you," she admitted with a guilty grin.

"I thought so. Come on, let's talk on the swing."

Sarah brushed the clayish dirt off her knees and hands and followed her mother up the steps. "Actually, there are two things."

"Sarah, I know we dropped a couple bombshells on you yesterday. We only intended to drop the one about the baby, and we had hoped to break the news to you and your sister under better circumstances . . ."

"I didn't know you wanted another baby, Mom. I mean, you never said anything."

"David and I want to have a child together – just like your father and I wanted you and Allison. You can understand that, can't you?"

"Yes, I guess so, but why so soon?"

"I know it seems rushed, but the main reason is my age. I'm 35 years old. I can't put off having a baby too much longer. And Sarah, I may as well tell you now; we may decide to have a second child."

"Gee, Mom, we'll be poor forever, and then I'll never get a horse." She tried to hold back the two fat tears welling up in each eye but she couldn't. Not wanting her mother to see, she quickly blinked them out and brushed them away.

Mrs. Conner leaned over and held Sarah close. "I promise you will get a horse before your thirteenth birthday."

"But I'm only eleven now. That seems so far away."

"Yes, but you'll be twelve in September, so we'll start looking seriously next summer. That won't be so bad now, will it?"

"I guess not."

"Now, what else did you want to ask me about?"

With a renewed sense of hope Sarah explained yesterday's escapade with Virgil and his job offer.

"Where is this farm?"

"I'm not sure exactly, but it's not far."

"Maybe we should first visit this farm and get acquainted. We'll have David call and see if Saturday morning is convenient."

"Really, Mom? You mean it?"

"It's worth looking into, and I think it would be a good experience for you."

"And I could pay David back without using too much of my savings."

"Honey child, with all the extra chores I've got lined up for you, you'll be adding money to that account!" teased Mrs. Conner.

"Thanks a lot, Mom!" Sarah nuzzled her mother playfully.

"Come on, let's go fix lunch- I'm starving!"

"Me, too. Mom, when will the baby be born?"

"Around the end of January or the beginning of February."

"So the spare bedroom's not for Grandma?"

"No, that'll be the nursery, and you get to help me decorate it!"

Following her mother into the kitchen, all Sarah could do was roll her eyes and shake her head. Thank goodness, their last name wasn't Hubbard.

*   *   *

Saturday morning, they drove the two and one half miles to the Reed farm. Just as Virgil had told David on the phone, it was the first farm past the railroad bridge; easy to reach on a one geared purple bike with rainbow streamers! A dusty clay-packed drive led them up a grassy knoll to a two story, white framed farmhouse, enclosed in a spacious front veranda and shielded by a gleaming tin roof. Two large swings hung on either side of the porch creaking and swaying in the light breeze, and in the middle sat three sturdy rocking chairs; each separated by a doily covered end table.

In the background, a weathered red barn roosted between a chicken coop and an odd assortment of splintery sheds housing a hodgepodge of farm machinery and peculiar looking implements. Off in the hilly distance, grew row after row of leafy green corn, their golden tassels rustling a soft lullaby in the breeze. To the right, was a great expanse of rolling pasture tumbling down to a deep flowing creek that snaked its way through a thick patch of woods.

It was love at first sight for Sarah and the Reed farm, affectionately named "Fond Acres," and it gave her the feeling of coming home after a long and tiring journey. Virgil and Virginia (Ginny, for short), were waiting expectantly on the porch when they pulled up. Introductions were made as Ginny offered everyone a sampling of her homemade raisin cinnamon rolls, coffee and orange juice.

"These are absolutely delicious," raved Mrs. Conner. "Could I ask for the recipe?"

"Surely. It was my mother's specialty before it was mine," said Ginny modestly.

Through the course of the conversation, the Conners learned that Ginny, who had never married, was the family care taker.

"Yessiree, whenever there's a new youngin or a sick relative, you'll find Ginny right there taking care of things," bragged Virgil. "She's a regular Florence Nightingale!"

Ginny blushed and shrugged Virgil off with a wave of her calloused hand. "Hush now, Virgil! There's no need to carry on so!"

Ignoring her with a fond wink, Virgil continued. "After our parents passed on, Ginny bounced around to whoever was in need. Then when my dear wife departed this world, Ginny moved in to help me through my grief, and she's been with me ever since – goin' on five years now. Lord help me, I don't know what I woulda done without her!"

"Somebody's got to keep you on the straight and narrow, baby brother," teased Ginny shyly.

"Truer words were never spokin'," laughed Virgil, as he stood up and brushed the crumbs off his overalls. "I reckon we ought to commence with the purpose of this here visit. Sarah here, needs to earn a fair sum of money, and me an' Ginny could use a little extra help three or four days a week. How's that so fer?"

"Right on track," agreed Mrs. Conner.

"Last evening, we composed a list of chores Miss Sarah could help us with since our backs ain't what they used to be."

"Truer words were never spoken!" chuckled Ginny.

"Here, sister, you read it. I left my reading spectacles on my nightstand."

Ginny cleared her throat politely before beginning. "Work in the vegetable garden…"

"Them green beans reproduce like wild rabbits," added Virgil. "I can't keep up with 'em."

"Muck out the stalls once a week…"

"Now that job's gonna be the hardest and the smelliest. The other days ya jest scoop up the piles of manure – don't worry, I'll show ya," added Virgil.

"Feed the chickens and gather the eggs." Ginny paused and waited. With a bemused smile, she continued. "Exercise Stormy."

"He'll need a good ride everyday yer here. Ya think ya can handle that?" asked Virgil with mock seriousness.

"Yes sir!" Sarah breathed a sigh of relief. He hadn't forgotten to include Stormy.

"Run errands to the store," Ginny continued patiently.

"Ginny here, prefers not to drive," explained Virgil. "It's not that she can't, mind ya, she jest prefers not to."

"Sarah's an expert at running errands," chimed Allison to the amusement of her family.

"And whenever the need arises, Sarah can help me with my canning, help Virgil mend fences and keep the tack clean and oiled."

"What about milking the cows?" asked Allison.

"Little miss, while them pretty blue eyes of yers are still fast asleep, ole Virgil's already up and milkin', but if ya like, I'll give ya a lesson this very day!"

"Can I, Mom, Can I?"

"Sure, honey, let's all have a lesson."

"If you folks don't mind, I'll get back to my pickling. Virgil, why don't you give them a little tour of the farm?"

"Splendid idea, big sister. How about it, folks?"

"We'd love to," answered David, as Sarah and Allison, remembering their manners, mouthed a silent but emphatic YES!

As Sarah entered the dimly lit barn, it reminded her of the manger scene with the Baby Jesus. All around, strands of morning sun filtered through the crevices, filling the air with a radiant glow. Whiffs of freshly cut hay and straw wafted down from the loft above to where it lay in fluffy heaps in the stalls below. There were three stalls on each side Inside two of them stood a pair of nearly identical ponies.

"This here is Stormy, the one ya helped lasso," reminded Virgil, "and this here is Stormy's mama, Blackie. She's as sweet as sugar, but she's getting' on in years, like ol' Virgil, aren't ya, girl?"

The other stalls were occupied by very fat milk cows. "Why are those cows so fat?" asked Allison.

"They're gettin' ready to drop their calves any day now."

"Why do they drop them? Doesn't that hurt?"

"That means they're going to have their babies very soon," explained Mrs. Conner, trying to conceal her amusement.

"Boy, you can sure tell you were raised in the city," quipped David good naturedly.

"So that means Mom is going to drop a baby!"

"No, you're mother is going to deliver a baby, silly!"

"So yer gonna have a new sister or brother! Ain't that grand!" congratulated Virgil.

"Yeah, wonderful," muttered Sarah under her breath.

"Are ya ready, then, fer yer first milking lesson?"

"I think so," stammered Allison, now that she was face to face with Dolly.

"Don't you fret, little miss. Dolly's as gentle as a lamb," reassured Virgil.

After a few awkward moments followed by several squeamish squeals and slippery mishaps, they each pumped and squeezed Dolly's teats, producing a thin stream of milk. When it was David's turn, he amazed his new family with his rhythmic expertise. Using both hands, the milk whizzed and pinged as it foamed into the shiny pail.

"If ya ever want a part-time job, Mr. Conner, jest let me know!"

"Where'd you learn to milk like that?" asked Mrs. Conner.

"I spent a few summers hanging around my uncle's farm. It's just like riding a bike. Once you learn, you never forget. David stood up revealing a half bucket of creamy white milk.

"Who's ready fer a pony ride?" asked Virgil with a gleam in his eye.

"All right!" cried Sarah. She wasn't expecting an invitation to ride and her heart raced with excitement.

"Little miss, you can ride Blackie, and Sarah can ride Stormy. Have ya done much riding, missy?"

"I used to take lessons and go on trail rides once a month at a ranch in Florida.

"Only once a month?"

"It was kind of far away, so a bus took a group from my school. We had to do all the work, too, like grooming and saddling and bridling our horse for the day. Sometimes we had relay races and games on horseback. It was so much fun." Sarah sighed, remembering those carefree Saturdays.

"Good you've got some experience under your belt 'cause Stormy needs a firm hand."

Behind the barn was a large, somewhat dilapidated riding ring. "My daughter used to practice in this here ring with Blackie a long time ago. I keep it tended, but it ain't been used fer a long time," said Virgil with a tinge of sadness. Then brightening he added, "It'll be good havin' a youngin' make use of it again."

While Blackie plodded along at a slow steady pace, Sarah struggled with Stormy. The obstinate pony started with a halting stiff walk, then proceeded to an uneven, bumpy trot and finally finished with an erratic canter. As she rounded the ring for the third time, she reined him to the gate where he lurched to a stop. "He sure is bouncy," she said breathlessly.

"He's jest workin' the kinks outta his system. He don't get ridden enough, so he's a mite unruly at the start. He'll settle down once ya start ridin' him regular. Down deep he's got a heart o' gold, don't ya boy?" Virgil's voice trailed off as he stroked Stormy's velvety muzzle. "Now, how 'bout that tour? We'll round up Duke and Edna and be on our way, lickety split."

Sarah pinched up her nose in puzzlement. "Who are Duke and Edna?"

"They're my mule team over in the next pasture."

Virgil and David led the ponies down a sloping hillside to a small pond. There stood Duke and Edna, both faded brown with long jack rabbit ears, taking a midmorning nap under a shady maple tree. Their eyes opened in unison as the group approached, and they greeted everyone with low friendly grunts. Snapping on a couple frayed halters with makeshift reins, Mr. and Mrs. Conner shared Duke's strong back and Virgil led the way on reliable Edna.

"What do you do with all that corn?" asked Allison.

"You sure ask a lot of questions," chided Sarah.

"Oh I sell some and eat some and feed my livestock some, so with all them mouths to feed, it don't last long," chuckled Virgil.

They rode on to the woods and followed the well-traveled deer path down to the creek, splashing through a glassy shallow section. "This here's a great swimmin' hole if ya'll ever wanna take a dip," offered Virgil. "And over here's a sweet alfalfa patch. Whenever Stormy runs off, this is the first place I check and sure enough, that's where he is, most times. The grass is always greener on the other side, ain't it boy."

"This creek looks like it goes for miles," remarked Mrs. Conner.

"Yer right there. It divides the pastures from the woods. We can't bring these critters here without letting graze a moment on this here delicacy. They'd pout fer days on end!"

While Stormy greedily ripped the tender shoots, Sarah walked to the creek's edge and took off her shoes and socks. "I better warn ya; that water is downright freezing till ya get used to it."

"It's like ice water." Sarah's teeth chattered as she felt the smooth stones beneath her feet.

"Be careful, missy. Them rocks area as slippery as ice cubes, too." But Virgil's warning was a second too late.

Everyone watched as Sarah slid down to her neck and popped up sputtering and shivering!

"You'll dry off in no time. I myself have slipped into that crick more times than I care to remember!"

Still dripping, Sarah mounted Stormy feeling like a total fool, but once back in the sunlight, she was nearly dry when they finished the ride. During the tour, her schedule was arranged and agreed upon. Every Monday, Wednesday and Friday morning, weather permitting, she would ride her bike to the farm. If she missed a day or had no other family plans, she could also work on Saturday.

Before Sarah went to bed that night, she recorded her topsy-turvy week in her diary. "Life is definitely improving," she wrote, as she finished her last entry.

Chapter Six

Farm Life

Sarah, who relished sleeping late all summer, woke before dawn fully awake. Scrambling out of bed, she swiftly dressed and tiptoed down the stairs in her socks. Everyone else was still asleep; even the house, she thought, smiling to herself, as she scanned the pantry shelves for a quick quiet breakfast. During the day, when the house was wide awake, small sounds escaped without notice. Now the walls were large amplifiers and every teensy weensy noise, like the plastic wrapped donuts, seemed to break the sound barrier. Exasperated, she jerked the stubbornly sealed package, sending a dozen powdered donuts airborne. Like a slow motion movie, they soared, then plummeted to their doom below. Some casualties lay in pieces on the floor while others, only dented, showed definite signs of life and were carefully replaced. Examining the broken sections, Sarah blew on them and remembering something her mother frequently said; "a little dirt never hurt anybody." She stuffed the limp remains in her mouth.

Pedaling down the sidewalk, Sarah realized she'd never been out this early before – *not early enough to beat the paper boy*, she thought, as she swerved to avoid an occasional newspaper that had missed its target. Slowly, the dark shade of night sky lifted to reveal the dim morning light while the streetlights blinked off one by one, their work finished for the night. Like a crowing rooster informing the world the day has begun, a wailing child from a nearby window, a barking dog and a rattly green pickup truck shattered the peaceful solitude. It was a new day and for once, Sarah was awake to be part of it. Pedaling faster now, she gained enough speed to ride easily up the railroad bridge, then coasted down to Virgil's entrance. Walking her bike up the grassy knoll, she saw him carrying two pails of frothing milk from the barn to the back of the house.

"I didn't expect ya here this early, missy!" he exclaimed, setting the pails on the back steps.

"I just woke up early for some reason!" she replied, shrugging her shoulders.

"It's better to clean them stalls while it's still a mite coolish. Ya ready to muck 'em out?"

"I guess so. I'm not really sure how to do it."

"It's kinda messy, but ya git used to it after a spell," said Virgil, grabbing two pitchforks.

The fermenting odor of urine and manure startled Sarah's nostrils the way her mother's cleaning ammonia did. "Pewy!" She rubbed her nose but it didn't help.

"In a few weeks, ya won't even notice that smell!" laughed Virgil. "Now, the first thing we do is shove the old muck outta the stalls and pile it up on that old wagon beside the door. That'll put muscle in yer arms right quick."

"Then what?" asked Sarah, trying to breath only through her mouth.

"I haul it to my compost pile to rot – the crops love it. Makes great fertilizer. But first, we hose out the stalls, let 'em dry and then sprinkle lime down for sanitizing. And after that, we finish up with a fresh bed of straw."

"How long does all that take?" asked Sarah dismally, thinking it would take up most of the day.

"Only a couple hours. And while them stalls are a dryin', we'll have ourselves a second breakfast."

"A second breakfast? How come?"

"Wait till yer finished mucking out – you'll understand then," chuckled Virgil.

At eight-thirty, Sarah felt as dirty and foul as the pile of muck on the wagon. Her fingers were stiff as Popsicle sticks and her arms, shaky as jello. Suddenly a loud bell was ringing, and she figured she was dizzy with hunger.

"That's Ginny, telling us to come and get it! Ya hungry yet?"

"Ravenous!" she gasped.

"Let's get ourselves washed up, then. Ginny won't tolerate us in her kitchen smellin' like a soiled stall!"

A bar of soap, an old black hand-pump and a fluffy towel produced near-miraculous results and as soon as Sarah and Virgil wiped their muddy shoes, they were allowed inside. A stack of blueberry pancakes with steaming syrup and a slab of crispy bacon evaporated as Sarah practically inhaled her second breakfast.

"Careful, Dear. You'll get a terrific case of hiccups if you gulp your food," cautioned Ginny.

"I don't think I've ever been this hungry before!" exclaimed Sarah, stopping to catch her breath.

"Farm work'll give ya an appetite, that's fer sure!" agreed Virgil, sopping up the last puddle of syrup on his plate.

"Ya'll rest a spell before riding that pony. Heaven forbid, Sarah get a bellyache and throw up," heeded Ginny, as she headed out the back door with a basket of wet laundry.

"Let's sit on the porch and let our food settle," suggested Virgil, as they ambled through the family room.

Following behind, Sarah noticed a photograph on the mantle; that of a smiling girl about her age astride a sleek black pony. "Is this the daughter that used to ride in the ring?" she asked.

"Yep, that's my Linda on Blackie. The two of 'em rode together in many a show. They was quite a team back then," he answered proudly.

Next to it was another photo of a woman standing with Linda, who clutched a first place trophy. "Is this your wife?" Sarah blurted out without thinking.

"That it is, missy. My dear departed Ophelia." Virgil's voice trembled slightly.

Remembering it was impolite to pry, Sarah asked no more questions.

"Say would ya like to see Linda's bedroom? I've saved all her mementos," invited Virgil.

"Okay," said Sarah, not sure what a memento was.

"This was her bedroom afore she left fer college," explained Virgil, as he opened the door revealing a roomful of trophies, ribbons and framed pictures. Sarah's mouth opened wide but she was speechless. "I'm right proud of my little girl, 'cept she's all growed up now."

"She won all these on Blackie?" asked Sarah in disbelief.

"Most of 'em."

"Does she still show horses?"

"No, but I'm hopin' she will again someday."

"Who taught her how to ride so well?"

"Who do ya think?" teased Virgil, his eyes twinkling like St. Nick's.

"Oh Virgil, would you teach me to ride like Linda?"

"Lemme think on that, missy. It's been near fourteen years since I coached Linda. Speakin' of ridin', ya ready to take Stormy fer a spin?"

"I was born ready!" she said.

In a matter of minutes, Sarah mounted one bewildered pony; this time ready for his balking and bucking. For nearly thirty minutes in the ring, Sarah showed Stormy who was boss.

"I think he's through arguing with ya," hollered Virgil. "Take him fer a run in the pasture and when yer done, walk him down to the crick for a drink, then turn him loose."

Coaxing the lazy grass-bellied pony into a canter took much clucking and kicking, but finally Stormy shifted his gears and broke into a slow comfortable canter. With a soft breeze blowing across her face, Sarah felt a sense of floating freedom. Cleaning out those nasty stalls had been worth it, she decided blissfully. Wishing this feeling could go on forever, but knowing it couldn't, she slowed Stormy to a trot, then a walk. She glanced at her watch, surprised at the time. It was only ten-thirty. *It seems like a whole day has passed by.* But a whole day was far from over, and she spent the rest of the morning picking buckets of tender green beans, early peas and bright yellow squash. Ginny had given her a little stool, but all that bending made her back sore after a while. So she switched from the stool to her knees, and then she tried scooching around on her bottom. At noon, she ate her snack, and soon after, Ginny sent her home with a bag of garden vegetables.

"You look plum wore out, Sarah," remarked Ginny. You'll most likely be sore tomorrow."

"Yessiree, ya did a fine job today, missy. A body never knowed it was yer first day," complimented Virgil.

As much as Sarah had enjoyed her first day, she was glad to go home. She was so tired her bones hurt and her over worked muscles felt as wobbly as a plate of noodles.

"You stink!" Allison held her nose when Sarah came through the front door.

"What did you expect, silly?"

"I'll run you a nice hot bath," suggested Mrs. Conner. "It looks like you've had quite a workout today."

"I did, but I had a great time," beamed Sarah, as she peeled off her sweaty clothes.

Easing into the warm tub reminded Sarah of a snug toasty blanket on a cold winter morning from which she never wanted to emerge. But twenty minutes later, Allison opened the bathroom door and shouted through the foggy vapor, "Mom said to get out before you turn into a prune!"

When it was time for dinner, Sarah trudged to the table. "I'm so tired, I think I might fall asleep right here." But her appetite proved stronger, and she ate two helpings of everything before dessert.

"Your arms will build up more strength in a couple weeks," reassured David. "I had the same problem years ago when I took a summer job at a construction site."

Shortly after dinner, Sarah crawled wearily into bed even though it was still light outside. By the time her head touched the pillow, she was fast asleep.

As David had predicted, Sarah's muscles developed along with a smooth routine. After her early morning chores, she rode Stormy before the heat of the day set in. The first few rides were bumpy and somewhat unpredictable, but very soon the pair became good friends, as they explored the wooded trails, pastures and dusty dirt roads. When the day came that Stormy answered Sarah's call and trotted eagerly to the fence, she knew for certain he looked forward to their rides as much as she did.

Then, unexpectedly one morning, Virgil hollered from the barn, "Ready fer yer first lesson, missy?"

"You mean you'll do it?" asked Sarah gleefully.

"I been watchin' ya ride and yer handling Stormy jest fine."

"Am I good enough to ride in a show?" she wondered.

"With enough practice, I expect so. There is one problem. . ."

"What is it?" she interrupted, a note of worry rising up.

"Don't fret, missy. It's not you. It's Stormy. He's never been shown before, and he's as spoiled as an overgrown pup He'll need an awful lot of training."

"He'll behave for me," she answered confidently. "Are there any shows around here?"

"As I recall, there's one in September during the Labor Day fair."

"What do we have to do to get ready? Let's get started!" bubbled Sarah.

"Hold on a minute, youngin'," laughed Virgil. "One step atta time. We'll start with the basics. Go saddle up his royal highness and meet me in the ring."

"I've never been to a horse show before. What events should I enter?"

"Best to keep Stormy in the Western classes. He's not cut out fer that fancy English style like Blackie was."

"Will we be ready by September?"

"I expect so, long as ya pay close attention and concentrate. We'll start ya off in the horsemanship class where the judge is watchin' how ya ride. That's not to say the horse doesn't matter now; 'cause he does. He has to behave in the ring with them other horses and do what ya tell him the instant ya give the command."

"What does the judge look for?"

"He's watchin' to see if yer a sittin' up straight and if yer hands and feet are jest right. Mount up and I'll show ya." Virgil had Sarah mount and dismount six times before he was satisfied. "That judge'll be watchin' how ya get on and off," he added.

The first week of training was strenuous. There were many details to remember, and Sarah had to think about every part of her body; something she'd never done before.

"Never take an ungroomed horse to a show," declared Virgil, the following day.

"You know I brush Stormy every day I'm here," reminded Sarah.

"That's true, missy, but only fer a few minutes. Starting today, ya gotta put in thirty whole minutes."

"Thirty minutes? I don't even spend that much time on myself," she protested.

"Ya wanna catch the judge's eye, don't cha?"

"Yes."

"The best way to do that is with a clean shiny coat that gleams in the sunshine. Add some linseed oil to his feed. That'll make his coat as smooth as silk, and the day before the show we'll give him a shave and a haircut!"

The thought of rough and tumble Stormy being pampered made Sarah and Virgil laugh aloud together. "I wonder what he'd say if he could talk," giggled Sarah.

"He'd make a fuss jest like a little boy who don't wanna come in fer a bath."

*   *   *

Sarah's days lasted much longer now. Besides the daily grooming and riding practice, she had her regular chores at the farm and at home. Her mother and David had approved the new routine provided Sarah could handle the extra responsibility. If she faltered, complained or whined, the show lessons would cease. Her time was strictly budgeted now that she visited the farm five to six days a week, but rather than tire her, the hectic pace filled her with excitement and anticipation. As her lessons progressed, the Western seat became second nature to her, and she often corrected herself if her reins were too high or her heels weren't low in the stirrups.

"I'm glad to see ya fixin' yer ownself," praised Virgil. "Means yer getting' the feel of it."

"I didn't think you saw me!" blushed Sarah.

"I don't miss too much!" winked Virgil.

One sultry afternoon, while Sarah was grooming Stormy in the barn, a small blue car pulled into the front yard. Out of it stepped an attractive young woman wearing jeans and a pink T-shirt. Pausing at the barn door, she asked Sarah, "Is Virgil here?"

"He went to the feed store, but he should be back soon," answered Sarah politely.

"I have an appointment, so I can't really wait long," she said, looking at her watch. "You must be Sarah. I'm Virgil's daughter, Linda."

"Did Virgil tell you about me?" asked Sarah, who felt awed by Linda's presence.

"Well, not exactly. Ginny mentioned that you were helping out and riding Stormy when I called last week," she replied in a slightly agitated tone.

"Yeah, I'm practicing for the Labor Day show. We want to win as many ribbons as you and Blackie did, don't we boy?"

"Since I won all my ribbons on Blackie, wouldn't you rather ride her? She's much easier to handle and already used to the show ring," suggested Linda

"No, Blackie's too slow now that she's older. And besides, I love Stormy." Sarah said, leading him towards the door. Linda quickly stepped back as Stormy came closer.

They talked a few more minutes about Sarah's family and then Linda said, "Well, it was nice meeting you, Sarah. I have to go now, but I'll stop by again later."

"Okay, see ya later," said Sarah. "I wonder what she wanted," she mumbled to herself. Without giving this visit a second thought, she resumed her grooming.

The afternoon was hot, and she'd promised Allison that morning she'd take her swimming at the college pool. Ginny usually took a short nap about this time of day, so Sarah gathered her things and quietly rode home. The humidity was heavy but it didn't dampen her spirits.

Thank -you, God!. It doesn't really matter that Stormy isn't officially mine. He's mine in my heart and that's all that matters.

This way was better, she told herself, because it didn't cost her any money, just honest hard work that she could supply much easier than cash! Soon, she'd work off her debt to David and then she could start saving for a show outfit.

Parking her bike in the yard, she could smell a stew simmering on the stove as she tromped up the wooden porch stairs. "Is that you, Sarah?" her mother called from the kitchen.

"It's me all right! Is Allison ready to go swimming?"

"No, I sent her next door to play with Lindsay."

"I'll go get her. She's been begging me to take her to the pool for a week."

"That can wait. Come sit down," her mother said somberly.

"Is anything wrong?" asked Sarah, who tried to think of anything she'd done to be reprimanded for.

"I'm afraid so."

This must be bad, thought Sarah. "Uh, did I do something wrong?" she stammered.

"No, sweetheart, you didn't," her mother said, wiping her hands on the dish towel that seemed glued to her shoulder. "But a serious situation has come up that we need to discuss."

"Are we moving away?" she gasped suddenly.

"No, it's nothing like that. Have a seat, Sarah," said David, patting the cushioned chair.

Sarah sat slowly and reluctantly.

"We got a call a little while ago from Virgil's daughter, Linda," explained David.

"Oh, she came by the farm today. Why did she call?"

"She's concerned that you're riding Stormy," continued David.

"Why?" chortled Sarah. "That's the silliest thing I've ever heard."

"Linda feels Stormy is too unruly for a girl of your age and experience," her mother said.

"Is this for real? She's crazy! Stormy is frisky, but he's not mean. He does everything I ask him. He wouldn't hurt a fly!" cried Sarah in disbelief.

"Linda feels very strongly that he's high strung and skittish."

"How would she know?" defended Sarah angrily. Sensing what was about to happen, her throat suddenly felt as if it were in a vice grip. "She doesn't live there anymore, she doesn't even ride anymore!"

"Linda has known Stormy since the day he was born. She helped raise him, Sarah," her mother tried to explain.

"She's just jealous because I can handle Stormy, and she never could! She only rode Blackie - dull, boring Blackie!" retorted Sarah.

"Sarah, your mother and I want you to ride Blackie from now on," said David, softly but firmly.

"You've seen me ride Stormy! Did he look dangerous? I've been riding him almost every day and nothing has happened! You guys are being paranoid over nothing! And besides, Virgil wouldn't let me ride him if he wasn't safe," exploded Sarah in one mad breath.

"Virgil may not realize,"

"What do you mean, Mom?"

"Well, maybe Stormy behaves for Virgil because he knows Virgil is the boss. You know a lot of dogs are like that. They only listen to one member of the family. Linda must have seen another side of Stormy's personality that Virgil isn't aware of."

"Virgil left me alone today and nothing happened." Sarah's words fell cold and hard like hailstones pelting the ground.

"Yes and we're glad, but as your parents, we have to do what we think is in your best interest. So for now, you'll have to ride Blackie," David repeated.

"That's not fair!" bellowed Sarah. "You're punishing me for nothing! And you're not even my father!" she added cruelly.

"In fairness to you and Virgil, I'll call him tonight and discuss it," agreed David. "But you have to realize, Sarah. . ."

Sarah didn't want to hear anymore. With a rush of raging tears blinding her eyes, she bolted from the kitchen and stomped up the stairs where she slammed the bedroom door loud enough for the neighbors to hear. Throwing herself on the bed, she buried her face deep into her pillow and cried hard, almost as hard as when her father died. Soon her eyes were red and puffy. Her nose was as stuffed as a Thanksgiving turkey forcing her to gulp air in through her mouth. Why was this happening? Why did Linda have to call and ruin her life? *I hate her, I hate her!* She tried to sit up but exhaustion and hunger forced her back to the wet tear stained pillow where she fell into a fitful sleep filled with strange and unpleasant dreams.

Chapter Seven

Shattered Dreams

Later that evening, Sarah woke up hesitantly, like an apprehensive child attempting the high dive for the very first time. Blinking open her swollen eyelids and feeling the dimness around her, she knew several hours had passed. Her eyes closed and she shuddered, sending a ripple across the spread that covered her. Outside, evening songbirds trilled a last lullaby before tucking themselves in for the night. *I wish I was a bird* fluttered like the wings of a hummingbird inside her throbbing head. As she laid there, her tired eyelids still resting, the sun vanished from the sky signaling the chirping to cease. There in the darkening shadows, confusing thoughts replaced the fluttering like taunting fireflies; flashing in front of you one second, then beside you, then behind and on and on until you were dizzy. *God I thought things were crazy before, but this! This doesn't make any sense – like Daddy dying. There's no reason for it. Lord, why would You give me a pony to ride and then let Linda come along and ruin it?*

Two large tears squeezed out of her clenched eyes, dripping steadily down the side or her cheeks before joining their fellow tear-mates on the pillow. *Why are the things I love taken from me? Will I ever understand, God?* But the only reply that reached her ears was the hum of the clock on the nightstand. Even that made her head ache. She rolled away, groaning. *And why did I have to go and say that to David? He probably hates me now. If only I could take it back. . .* He didn't deserve it, but the words had spilled out of her like a knocked over glass of milk and this was one spill she was crying over.

Her bedroom door creaked open. "Are you awake, Sarah?" her mother whispered.

"Sort of," she croaked back.

"Want some dinner?"

"No, thanks. Not hungry," she forced out. Each word felt as rough and heavy as a brick, making the least bit of conversation arduous and tiring.

"I brought you a bowl of chicken noodle soup. You sure you wouldn't like some?" she persuaded.

"I'll spill it," she replied wearily.

Being a nurse and a mother, Mrs. Conner always knew how to make a body feel better – whether or not it wanted to or not. "Lean forward," she said, fluffing and propping the mashed pillows.

Too numb to argue, Sarah obliged her.

"Comfy?"

Sarah nodded.

"Here's a napkin." She spread it across Sarah's chest, tucking the top edge under her collar. "Here you go," she said aiming the spoon towards Sarah's closed moth.

The soup smelled warm and inviting, and her mouth opened automatically like the doors at the grocery store. She swallowed slowly letting the soothing broth work its healing on her scratchy throat and churning stomach. Halfway finished, she faltered.

"Too hot?" asked her mother, blowing across the still steamy bowl.

"No, it's fine. I just wondered if David called Virgil yet."

"Yes, he called about an hour ago."

"Well, what did he say?" she asked anxiously.

"He respects our decision, of course."

"Is that all?" injected Sarah, who was hoping for a change in the decision.

"No, he said that Linda developed a terrible fear of horses shortly after her mother died. And he assured us that Stormy is a well-mannered pony who's just a bit spoiled, but he understood our concern."

"So, then it's okay for me to ride Stormy?" she reasoned, feeling a surge of relief.

"Well, no, not exactly."

"What do you mean, no, not exactly?" The relief was plummeting like a rock thrown off a cliff.

"I know how much this means to you, Sarah, I really do."

"No, you don't. If you did, you wouldn't be doing this to me." The tears broke through like a dam bursting.

"Sarah, please try to understand my point of view. If something happened to you that I could have prevented, I'd never be able to forgive myself."

"Yeah, but . . ." she protested.

"Maybe when you're a little older and more experienced, I'll reconsider it."

"How can I get any experience riding pokey old Blackie?" she sobbed.

"Give Blackie a chance. Don't forget about that roomful of ribbons and trophies," encouraged Mrs. Conner.

"That was a long time ago, Mom, when Blackie was young and strong, like Stormy is now," she tried to explain.

"With a little patience and training, I'll bet Blackie remembers everything."

"I doubt it," she mumbled miserably. There was no use arguing. She was licked and her mother wasn't budging.

The next morning she stayed in bed waiting for David to leave. As if she didn't have enough problems, she knew she had to apologize eventually but not right now. *Later on. Maybe before dinner. Maybe I'll feel almost human by then.*

That morning she pedaled so slowly, she had to walk her bike over the railroad bridge before coasting down to the farm. *This is so embarrassing! Why am I even going up here? I guess it's better than staying home sewing curtains for the nursery! Why is Mom so over-protective? Virgil's gonna think I'm some kind of ninny.*

Lost in her ranting, she was startled to hear Virgil's cheerful greeting. "What kinda look is that on sech a beautiful day?"

"Wouldn't you feel lousy if you couldn't ride your favorite pony anymore?" she groused.

"Yes, I suppose I would at that. But we gotta respect your parents' wishes, missy. They're only thinkin' of yer best interest."

Frustrated she blurted out, "Why is Linda so afraid of horses? I mean, she rode for years. I just don't get it!"

Virgil looked down and kicked a rock before answering. Without looking up, he answered, choosing each word carefully. "Sometimes people change when somethin' bad happens. Ya get what I'm sayin'?"

"I think so."

In a halting voice, Virgil tried to explain. "Linda's mother was killed by a colt and ever since, she won't go near a horse, not even her own beloved Blackie. That's all I can say about it, missy."

Stunned, Sarah felt ashamed complaining about her petty problems. She decided to try and make the best of things right then and there. Maybe Blackie would work out, after all. Attitude is everything, she recalled a teacher saying. Well, the least she could do was try. She followed Virgil to the barn where Stormy was hitched up to a small wagon.

"Since you'll be riding Blackie, Stormy'll be pulling the cart now and then. He sorely needs the practice. Think ya can handle ol' Blackie by yerself?" he chuckled good naturedly.

"Better yet, can Blackie handle me?" she joked back, trying to mask her disappointment.

Seeing them off she sighed, then headed out to find Blackie. Since she was older and out of shape, she would have to be reconditioned slowly, thought Sarah as she spotted the black mare grazing with Duke and Edna. "It's not that I don't like you," she explained to the docile pony. "You're very sweet, but you remind me of an old, faithful hound dog, instead of a show horse." She slipped the bridle on and decided to meander bareback through the fields rather than start training in the ring.

Blackie seemed to enjoy all the extra attention and started waiting at the fence for Sarah to take her out every day. It broke Sarah's heart to have to leave Stormy behind and when he whinnied after them, it was sheer torture. The daily workouts in the ring quickly proved to be futile. Blackie tried her very best, but it wasn't good enough. She was too slow and as much as Sarah hated to admit it, riding the sweet little mare was terribly tedious. "I guess that's why you and

Linda won so many ribbons together," she observed sadly. "You're so obedient and predictable, not like Stormy at all!"

That afternoon before she left for the day she told Virgil, "I can't show Blackie after all. She doesn't have enough stamina anymore."

"She is gettin' on in years," agreed Virgil, scratching his fuzzy white stubble.

"What am I going to do now?" Her voice wavered at the thought of missing the show.

"I wish I could give ya an answer to make ya feel better, missy. There'll be another show come April. Maybe by then, somethin' will work out."

"It's so unfair!" she pouted. Then, remembering her promise not to complain, she bit her lower lip and swallowed her anger.

"Don't let it getcha down, missy. Things have a way of working themselves out in due time," he consoled.

"Not for me, they don't," she groused.

"Ya gotta put yer situation in the Lord's hands. He knows what's best even if it don't make sense."

"What I can't figure out is," wondered Sarah, "is why God answered my prayer, and then He unanswered it."

"The Good Book says 'All things work together fer good to those who love God and keep His commandments.'"

"What does that mean, exactly?"

"Well, missy, I'm no preacher, but I done a heap a listenin' and it seems to me that the good Lord, He knows us better than we know our own selves. And it stands to reason that if we believe in Him and trust Him, He's gonna direct our path and guide our footsteps through thick and thin."

"But why do bad things have to happen?" sighed Sarah dismally.

"Oh, missy, that's a hard one. Folks been askin' that since Adam and Eve. I done a lot a thinkin' on that after my Ophelia went to her reward and the way I figure, is how can we really trust the Lord if nothin' bad ever happens? Wouldn't be no reason for havin' any faith at all."

"I guess so. But how does having faith help me?" asked Sarah.

"I heard someone say once that havin' faith makes you *better* instead of *bitter*. I kinda liked that so I tucked it up here under my hat!" winked Virgil.

"Yeah, I like that, too." She smiled faintly.

"Well, missy I gotta get back to my chores. Will I be seein' ya tomorrow, as usual?"

Sarah nodded, then said, "Thanks, Virgil. I'll try to remember what you said.

*   *   *

Heading home, she didn't quite comprehend everything, but most of it made sense, even though the trusting part seemed like an awfully hard thing to do. Still, she couldn't erase the image of Stormy riding in the Labor Day show. It hung around like a kid at a construction site drooling over scrap lumber. Then to add to her frustration, a text from Jennifer had arrived that afternoon:

Dear Sarah,

Love the pics of you & Stormy! He's so pretty! I'd give anything to watch you ride in the show. Please send more pics after you win your blue ribbon. We are going to the Grand Canyon, so I'll text you later.

Still your Best Friend, Jennifer!

What a bummer! How can I ever explain all this mess? At least, she'll be gone for a while, so I don't have to answer this right away. Maybe Jennifer would forget and she wouldn't have to explain.

She resumed her routine at the farm as best she could, but knowing there was no show future with Blackie left her feeling as fizzled out as a flat soda. Then one morning, as she pedaled up the dusty drive, she noticed Duke saddled and tied to the fence. "Are you taking Duke out today?" she asked half-heartedly.

"No, missy, he's a waitin' fer you."

"Me? What for?"

"Ol' Duke here, he's as gentle as a pussy willow, but he's a heap more fun to ride. I checked with yer Ma and she said okay."

"Well, I guess I could give him a try." Sarah was skeptical since even a goat would be more fun than Blackie.

"I'll be needing a favor from ya, too," said Virgil.

"Sure, Virgil. I may as well be useful."

"I'm a little shorthanded these next few weeks what with Ginny being gone to help our niece with her new baby and I sure would appreciate it if ya could deliver these bills on Duke," he said, handing her two envelopes. "This here's my grocery bill fer Mr. Fitch and this one's fer Harold at the hardware store. I'd go myself but you-know-who escaped last night and I gotta go round him up."

"That rascal! I bet he's in the alfalfa patch right now."

"I'd bet my bottom dollar yer right, missy."

"Can't he stay over there awhile and graze?" she asked. "Won't he come home on his own?"

"Alfalfa to Stormy is like candy to a youngin' A little is okay but too much'll give him a bellyache. That pony is just too smart fer his own good! When ya get back, we'll look fer the spot in the fence where he broke through."

"Okay, I'll be back soon," said Sarah, nudging Duke down the drive.

Duke was an easy-going mule and like Virgil said, was more enjoyable to ride. Being somewhat taller than the ponies, he had a comfortable rhythmic gait that mellowed Sarah's muddled mind. "Too bad there's not a show for mule riding!" She told Duke as they clip-clopped down the quiet road. She passed a park where a family was having a picnic and thought; *we ought to have a picnic at the farm! Virgil would enjoy the company while Ginny's away, Allison could ride Blackie, and I could show Mom how well I ride Stormy! Hey! What a great idea! I could show her and David how much I've improved! I'm so much better than that first day. No wonder Mom's worried.* She shook her head and chuckled to herself thinking back to that first rough ride. Stormy nearly bucked her off!

Spurring Duke on, she finished the errands quickly, so she could get back and launch her plan. "I'm back, Virgil, she shouted gaily, dismounting Duke,

"Yer in a chipper mood. Riding ol' Duke is good medicine fer the soul, I always say."

Not really listening, she babbled, "Would it be all right with you if my family had a picnic up here?"

"Sure, missy, that's be jest fine. You jest let me know when."

"Great. I'll ask them at dinner, tonight."

She went home bursting with the enthusiasm of a cheerleader. All she had to do was show them that she and Stormy now performed like a well-oiled machine instead of oil and water. They would be so impressed, they'd change their minds on the spot. The scene played out in her head like a movie: *Sarah, we are so impressed with your riding that we've decided to let you ride Stormy. It was very unfair of us to make such a harsh decision without first watching you ride. Will you forgive us?* And of course, she would, because they were only being parents, after all.

A picnic was arranged for the following Saturday. Setting it up had been a breeze, since they loved the idea the instant she suggested it.

"It's been awhile since we've done anything together," her mother had said.

"You're right, sweetheart. I'd like to speak with Virgil about his garden. I thought we might have one in the backyard next year," agreed David.

"Yeah, and I want to ride Blackie again," Allison managed between bites of ice cream.

Sarah only smiled.

*   *   *

Saturday dawned with a bright blue sky overflowing with puffy white clouds that resembled giant mutant vegetables and other sci-fi creatures. *It's a perfect day for a picnic*, she said to herself, gazing out the window. While dressing, she rehearsed her plan: *First, I'll go to the farm and help Virgil with the chores. Then, I'll get Blackie ready for Allison and Stormy for me. After lunch, she'll ride and then I'll surprise everyone, even Virgil.*

By one o'clock, the pieces of Sarah's puzzle were falling into place like clockwork. Allison was riding Blackie, and soon it would be time to present the new and improved Stormy! She could hardly wait!

"You're certainly in a good mood, today," observed her mother.

"She's been like this all morning," replied Virgil. "Like a whirlwind she was, a-going through her chores!"

As Virgil spoke, a low rumble vibrated across the sky. Then a small gust of wind scattered the napkins around the yard. Too excited to notice, Sarah ran into the barn to check on Stormy. "Just a few more minutes, boy, and we'll show them you're as harmless as a kitten."

The light filtering through the cracks in the barn wall suddenly disappeared, like a snuffed-out candle. Outside, she heard David calling, "Sarah, come get Blackie."

That's odd. Is Allison finished already? She ran out, the wind whipping harder now as dark ominous rainclouds advanced, devouring the few remaining patches of blue. Mrs. Conner and Allison were gathering the picnic remains while David helped Virgil tie down anything that might blow away. *This can't be happening! What am I going to do now?* Sarah's thoughts stuck together like a peanut butter and jelly sandwich as she pulled Blackie into her stall. Then Virgil rushed in muttering to himself. "Why is Stormy saddled up?" he asked impatiently.

Hastily, Sarah tried to explain.

"Can't ya see a storm is brewing, child? Get in the house, and I'll take care of Stormy!" he ordered sharply.

Sarah was stunned. Didn't he understand how important this day was? This might be her only chance before the show, and he didn't care. Fuming silently, she marched stiffly towards the house. *I only needed a few minutes. That storm won't be here for another hour at least. Why are adults such worry warts?"*

David hurried into the house, out of breath. "I think we can make it home before it hits. Did you close all the windows?"

"All closed," answered Mrs. Conner.

"Let's go then. I've said goodbye."

"Where is Virgil?" asked Allison, munching on a drumstick.

"He left to gather his calves. Boy, this really looks like a whopper of a storm coming in."

Tumbling into the car, Sarah snapped, "I don't see why we couldn't stay a little longer."

"What's eating you?" asked her mother. "You were in such a good mood, earlier."

"Just leave me alone," she muttered under her breath.

"When we get home, you can be alone in your room until you're in a civil mood," admonished her mother.

Upstairs, Sarah sat at her desk, intensely sketching plans of the horse farm she would someday own. At least then, she could ride any horse she wanted. Her farm would be the best for miles around. Everyone would want to board their horse at her stable. There would be a two story brick house on a hill overlooking acres and acres of lush Kentucky bluegrass. There'd be at least three barns with three riding rings, maybe even four. Beyond the pastures would be miles of twisting trails to explore through thick leafy woods ,and possibly a cave or two might be fun. Last, would be a real swimming hole for hot summer afternoons where she and her friends could have barbeques and make homemade ice cream. Sarah sat back, admiring her adult life. It would be wonderful. But for now, this future bliss would have to be filed away with all the others in the box under her bed. Heaving a heavy sigh, she plopped down on her bed, her thoughts turning to the day's events and her ruined opportunity. She'd have to come up with something else to prove her point, but what? Her mind was as blank as a school chalkboard in summer.

While she pondered her dilemma, she heard the sound of little pebbles chinking against the windowpane. That pesky boy from down the street surely couldn't be wanting Allison to come out and play now. Getting up to investigate, she was startled to see hard drops of rain crashing and splattering against the glass. She watched as the hard drops turned into a driving torrent, the water pounding the window with such ferocity, she was afraid the glass might break. The treetops creaked like a creaky wooden door and the wind moaned deeply, giving the room a spooky feeling, even though it was only three o'clock. Putting her own troubles aside, Sarah's concern shifted to Virgil and the animals. Suddenly, a sharp piercing crack shattered the air, sending shivers down her spine. Cupping her hands against the foggy window, she faintly made out a large oak branch lying in the yard. It had snapped like a toothpick from the thick trunk. For several hours, the storm raged with intense fury and when it was time for bed, all she could do was huddle under her covers as the bright lightning and booming thunder battled back and forth.

She must have drifted off eventually because a high pitched buzzing sound woke her in the morning. Looking out the window, she gasped as if the breath had been knocked out of her. The brilliant blue sky gave no hint of the war that had waged during the night, but the destruction below was evidence enough. The neighborhood looked as though it had been turned upside down and shaken long and hard. Their neighbor, Mr. Harrison was sawing the broken limbs into compact logs with his chain saw while his wife and kids bagged up the smaller twigs and matted leaves.

When she walked onto the front porch, she found her parents discussing the damage with some of the neighbors. "This was the worst summer storm we've had since I can remember," remarked one old timer.

"No, I think the one five years ago was worse. I thought my roof was gonna fly right off! But thank the Lord, it held. Had to replace quite a few shingles, though."

"We've got our work cut out for us today, that's for sure," said David grimly. "Better get into our work clothes."

All morning long, they raked and bagged the sticks, stalks, stems, acorns, leaves and litter. *We'll never finish*, thought Sarah, surveying the endless debris surrounding her. But after Mr. Harrison finished sawing the branches in his yard, he came over and started on the Conner's, which definitely improved the looks of things. As they stacked the wood against the garage, he joked, "We got enough firewood to last us through ten winters!"

At lunch, Mrs. Conner said, "Sarah, why don't you call Virgil and see how he's doing?"

"I'm sure he could use some help," added David. "Tell him we can come over this afternoon."

Sarah held her phone, fidgeting. Then nervously, she called, feeling both foolish and disappointed. The phone rang. It rang again. Ten rings later, there was still no answer. "No answer," she said, letting it ring a few more times. Virgil still used a house phone and didn't have voicemail.

"Well, I suppose he's out cleaning up just like we've been doing," reasoned David. "We'll try again later. I'll be out helping Wally cut up a few more downed trees."

"Sarah, why don't you ride up and see how Virgil fared," suggested her mother.

How could I be mad at Virgil? He didn't know about my plan. It was stupid to think he'd understand with a storm on the way. I should have called first thing this morning. Anxious to make up for lost time; she pedaled faster, a lump of nervous dread lodged in her throat. When she reached the drive, the lump slid down into the pit of her stomach and turned into a twisted knot. One side of the barn was caved in revealing a skeleton frame underneath. Fragments of every sort were strewn as far as her eyes could see. The corral was a pool of oozing mud with a twisted mangled fence hanging on for dear life. A peculiar stillness hung in the air, and the eerie silence was frightening. Her ears ached for a sound, even a bird or a bug, but all she heard was the pounding of her own heart.

Exploring further, she discovered the truck parked in what was left of the garage. Walking behind the barn, she saw Duke and Edna grazing in the swampy looking pasture. *He couldn't be running errands, not with his truck and Duke here.* **"Virgil!"** she shouted. The only answer that came was a halfhearted bray from Duke. With panic rising in her heart, Sarah ran, tripping and stumbling across the branch laden yard, to the front porch. Trying the unlocked doorknob, she pushed the stubborn door open. It creaked, then sagged like a damp sponge. "Virgil," she whispered nervously. The house was empty. Musty odors already permeated the walls and furniture. With goosebumps erupting up and down her arms, she opened a few windows. Like the door, the bulging sashes resisted, but with several firm tugs and grunts, she managed to lift up most of them, allowing the warm fresh air to circulate throughout the dark dank rooms. The exertion left her calmer, and she quickly checked the rest of the house. The bedroom looked exactly as it had yesterday, when she and her mother had closed the windows. Maybe the kitchen would reveal some clues as to Virgil's whereabouts. It was difficult to tell if anything had been used since he and Ginny were so tidy. She opened the refrigerator, remembering the leftovers her mother had placed inside, To her horror, the leftover picnic food sat untouched on the top rack where her mother had left it with a note:

Virgil,

Here are some leftovers for your dinner tonight.

Thanks for having us! Stay safe, Amy

The moist ink on the page ran down in smeary streaks. Her heart skipping a beat, she knew Virgil hadn't seen the note or eaten anything after the storm hit. *He never made it back to the house!* Bursting out the kitchen door, she uttered a cry when she saw the poor dead chickens in their coop. Virgil always let them out during the summer rains so they could seek better shelter in the barn. Why hadn't he let them out yesterday? Alarmed, she called home for help but there was no service. Leaving a rushed message on the voicemail, she ran back to the barn. A jolt of fear seized her. **"Virgil, where are you?"** she screamed.

Chapter Eight

The Aftermath

"I've got to find him! Dear God, please help me find him! And please let him be okay." Sarah prayed, shuddering at the thought of what she might find. "Stay calm and think clearly," repeating what her mother would say when she was frustrated with her math homework. "What to do, what to do…," she mumbled, making a quick inspection inside the barn. Stormy and Blackie were gone; their stall doors hung sideways with loose dangling hinges and dangerous protruding nails. Examining the lopsided doors, she realized they kicked and pushed their way out. "Poor things must have been scared to death," she said to Dolly, who stood in her flooded stall, looking hungry and forlorn. "Come on, girl. You can go outside and graze, she told the cow, leading the black and white Holstein outside. Duke and Edna kept grazing, but looked up when she opened the gate.

It was then Sarah noticed Duke's reins dangling at his feet. "Virgil must have used you to round up the calves. Here Duke, here boy," she called gently, her hand outstretched towards the grazing mule. Approaching cautiously, so as not spook him, Sarah remembered Virgil explaining once how, "it can take days fer some critters to settle down after a bad scare. Chickens won't lay, cows won't let down their milk and horses are plum half crazy!"

Stepping forward at a snail's pace, she carefully lifted the reins with one hand and stroked Duke on the neck with the other. "You don't feel tense. Nothing upsets you, Duke, as long as you can eat. But right now, you gotta take me to Virgil, you hear me?" she said, hoisting herself upon his mud caked back. It seemed logical to start in this field, but with all the pasture gates open, it was anybody's guess after that. Straining her eyes, she watched for any movement. Just as she was about to turn away, she spotted a rustle in the tall grass ahead. Spurring Duke on, he trotted forward. Suddenly, he shied sharply to the right nearly tossing her off, had she not instinctively slumped down and grabbed his withers. "What's the matter, boy?" The grass rustled again, revealing a small brown rabbit. Looking around timidly, his tiny gray nose twitching fretfully, he scampered away with his white cottontail bobbing behind. "Oh, brother. Is that what scared you? Come on now. We've got to find Virgil before it's too late." *No, don't think like that. He's okay, wherever he is, he's got to be okay.* After scanning the field anxiously for a few minutes, she kicked duke impatiently. "He's not here. Let's try the cow shed."

The cow shed sat at the bottom of a rolling hill nestled in a grove of shady trees. As Sarah approached it, she saw a large tree branch lying on the roof. One end was burned and charred, as was the jagged rip on the trunk from where the limb had grown. "Lightning must have struck it," she murmured, gulping at the sight of the disabled oak. Dismounting, she led Duke across the maze of branches and twigs, not taking any chances on his stumbling, despite his sure footedness. When she reached the door of the shed, she tied him to a front railing, then peeked inside, almost afraid of what she might find. Just as she had dreaded, there lay Virgil, crumpled over with blood smeared across his face. Rushing to his side so quickly, she thought she might faint, she prayed, "Dear God, *please* don't let him be dead." Leaning over, she tried in vain to hear a heartbeat. "Virgil? Virgil?" She cried fearfully. Moaning ever so softly, his eyelids fluttered briefly, then he lapsed back into unconsciousness. Filled with relief, she breathed a prayer of thanks. But every moment counted and as she rose, she saw a beam lying beside him. Looking up, there was a vacant gap in the ceiling from where it had fallen.

Years of eroding moisture had rotted the underside, and it only took a second to realize that when the lightning struck, the impact of the falling branch had knocked the beam loose, hitting Virgil on the head. She had to think fast as every minute was precious, but her head felt like a dribbling basketball in search of a hoop. There was no way to carry him back and in First Aid class, she'd been taught not to move an injured person. Hard as it was to leave him, she knew she had to get help *fast*! Bending down, she whispered in his ear, "Virgil, I'm going to go get help. Can you hear me? Don't worry, I'll be right back. You've got to hang on Virgil, do you hear?" Drowning in feelings of helplessness, Sarah left Virgil lying silently on the sodden dirt floor. On her way out, she snatched up a long thin branch and mounting Duke, applied a stinging whip to his rump. Feeling the urgency, Duke sprang forward, cantering all the way back to the house.

"I'm fine. It's Virgil. He's been hurt!"

"Where is he?"

"Down at the cow shed. Redialing her house number, she pleaded for someone to answer the phone. "Hello?" came Allison's high-pitched voice.

"Allison, go get Mom or David and ***hurry!***"

"Why? What's the matter?"

"Virgil's been hurt real bad. Now hurry!" she demanded.

"Sarah listened as Allison ran across the floor and slammed the screen door. In seconds, David was on the line. "David, you've got to get up here quick!" she panted.

"Sarah, slow down and tell me what happened. Are you alright?"

"Yes. A big beam fell and knocked him out and he's just lying there with blood on his face and I'm afraid he's gonna die!"

"Sarah, listen to me carefully. I'll call an ambulance. You wait for me on the front porch, so you can show us the way. Do you understand?" David's voice was strong but calm.

"Yes, I'll wait here for you. Just **hurry!**"

David arrived in less than ten minutes. Five minutes later, a siren wailed in the distance, growing louder as it approached the farm. Turning into the drive where they were waiting in the car, David shouted, "Follow us!" to the driver with a wave of his arm. With Sarah pointing the way across the mushy pasture, David parked under the trees while the ambulance driver parked next to the door. The paramedics rushed inside with a stretcher as Sarah and David waited nervously outside. A moment later, they expertly steered Virgil through the door and into the ambulance. David spoke with the driver briefly, while Sarah stood at a distance, numbly watching the whole scene. "Is he going to be all right?" she asked, her voice trembling.

"He's badly injured," said David, placing his arm around her shoulder as they returned to the car. "The medic said it was a good thing you found him when you did. He wouldn't have made it otherwise. I'm really proud of you."

Sarah was too choked up to speak.

"We need to find Linda's phone number to let her know what's happened."

Sniffing back tears, she nodded.

Together, they looked for Linda's number, but it wasn't in the phone book or any of the address books near the phone. "Too bad the internet's still down. I'll look through some of the other drawers," said David, thinking out loud. "Did Virgil happen to mention the name of the niece Ginny's visiting?"

"No, I don't remember him mentioning any name but hey! I almost forgot! Virgil has a desk in the barn where he does a lot of his paperwork. I'll go check out there," she said, running out the door.

"Good idea," David hollered after her. "I'll call your mother and let her know what's going on."

Virgil's desk, once a beautiful mahogany roll top, was now so aged and warped from the humid summers and wet winters, the top no longer rolled and two of the drawers seemed cemented shut. It was weathered and worn from years of faithful service and like Virgil, it wasn't fancy with ornate carvings but instead, stood steady and firm year after year. There were three drawers on each side and one in the middle. Beneath the roll top were lots of cubbyholes and compartments, all filled with smudged slips of paper, rusty paperclips, dried-out rubber bands and faded envelopes. Six handmade paperweights, each a grade school gift from Linda, sat upon six piles of bills and receipts. A veil of dirt and dust had settled permanently on the entire arrangement and despite the storm, the desk had stayed dry in the tack room.

Sarah hadn't ever paid much attention to the seasoned desk before and the paperweights distracted her momentarily from her search. She admired one, especially, since it reminded her of one she'd made in kindergarten. Chipped and cracked, the round plaster of paris mold held a child's small handprint and she smiled. *This one must be Virgil's favorite.* The thought of Virgil sent her fingers scurrying back to the unopened drawers. The first two on either side were business files. The other two that still opened contained an odd assortment of locks, keys, stubby pencils, small pieces of tack, hardware and some newspaper clippings. She lifted the clippings out and placing them on top of the desk, discovered in the back of the drawer, a small coverless address book. "I found something!" she exclaimed to David, who was hurrying towards the barn.

They quickly found the number, and Sarah listened grimly as David relayed the accident to Linda. When he hung up, he said to her, "Your mom and I are going to leave Allison with the Harrisons and meet Linda at the hospital."

"Can I go, too?" begged Sarah.

"I'm afraid not. Only family members can go into the intensive care ward. But I'll ask the doctor when you can visit after he's on the regular ward. I've locked the house. You go ahead and finish up here as best you can with the animals and head on home.

"Okay," she said dejectedly.

"Everything's gonna be all right, you'll see," soothed David. "You okay?"

"Yes," she sighed wearily. "David…"

"Yes, Sarah…?"

"I'm sorry about what I said awhile back – you know, about not being my father," she stammered.

"I know you didn't mean it, but I'm glad we cleared the air," he said warmly. "You're a good kid, Sarah, and if I could handpick a daughter, it'd be you."

"Thanks." She blushed and felt awkward now, but she wanted to tell him, too, what a great stepdad he was without being corny. "I'm glad Mom married you," popped out and that summed everything up like a neatly wrapped gift.

"So am I," winked David, as he got into the car. I'll see ya at home."

Nodding and waving goodbye, Sarah wandered back to the tack room. Seeing that she'd left the newspaper clippings out, she glanced at one and reading nothing of interest, turned the page over, revealing a startling story. The headline read, **"LOCAL WOMAN KILLED IN ACCIDENT WITH PONY."** Stunned, Sarah didn't have to read the article to know who the woman was. Being curious though, she read on. "Mrs. Ophelia Reed of Wilmore, died of head injuries inflicted by the family's two year old colt. Seventeen year old daughter, Linda Reed, explained that the pony became frightened during yesterday's thunderstorm, reared up and struck Mrs. Reed, as she attempted to lead the pony to his stall. Mr. Reed was unavailable for comment. Funeral services will be held this Sunday at the United Methodist Church on East Main Street at two o'clock." Shocked by the details, Sarah had to sit down to think through all she'd just read. The article was five years old. The pony had been a two year old colt at the time of the accident and would now be seven. Stormy was seven. Could he be the colt that had reared up and killed Mrs. Reed? She desperately hoped not, but she had a sinking feeling her suspicions were correct.

Another clipping lay on the desk. Hoping it might reveal more clues, she searched for information, but could only find one story intact. It didn't relate to Mrs. Reed's death, but Sarah read it anyway. **UNKNOWN GOOD SAMARITAN SAVES CHILD DURING STORM.** "An unidentified man stopped his truck during yesterday's thunderstorm to aid a woman in distress. Said Mrs. Richards of Wilmore, 'I lost control of my car and skidded into a ditch. My boy was eating a piece of candy, and it must have stuck in his throat when the car landed in the ditch. He was choking and turning blue, and I couldn't get it out when this nice man stopped and helped me. He saved my son's life, but he hurried away before I could thank him. All I know is he was older, had a thick white beard and drove a blue truck. My husband and I would like him to come forward, so we can show him our gratitude.'"

Virgil's truck is red, but it could have been blue and, he doesn't have a beard, but he's got thick white hair. Hmm, it could have been him, she reasoned. *No, I'm sure of it.* Placing the two articles side by side, she proved to herself she was right. First of all, the dates were identical, second, both referred to 'yesterday's thunderstorm,' and both had been cut out and saved by Virgil. Shaking her head in amazement, she stared at the tattered yellow clippings.

Outside, trotting hooves and a high piercing whinny startled her. Jumping up, she bounded outside. "Blackie! Where have you been, girl? Look at you! You're a mess!" Blackie's mane and tail were tangled and snarled with prickly thorns and stubborn burrs. Her coat, like Duke's, was caked with mud, and her legs were scraped with several cuts, some deep, on her chest and sides. The usual sedate pony was a mass of quivering flesh, and it took much coaxing to get her into the safety of a semi-dry stall. Sarah spoke gently and watched as the unsettled pony paced and turned before finally settling down. She fixed this stall with fresh straw and a bit of hay, then lured her in with a can of oats. *What could have happened? And where is Stormy?* He was always running away, but this time it was different. There had been a terrible storm, like the one five years ago that ended tragically. Her head hurt, and she was confused. *What should I do?* Now that

Blackie was settling down, she thought it best to clean her wounds and dab some ointment on them. The next step followed logically: *I've got to find Stormy!*

Chapter Nine

Search and Rescue

"You tried to follow Stormy, didn't you, girl?" said Sarah, carefully applying some first aid cream to Blackie's scrapes. "You rest now, and we'll call the vet after I find Stormy."

Grabbing Stormy's bridle and a long rope (every rescue scene on TV usually involved a long rope) she decided to hike down to the alfalfa patch. But remembering David's words to hurry home, she left him a voice mail and then tacked a hastily scribbled note on the front door in case the phones were down again.

David,

Blackie came back after you left but Stormy is still gone. I've gone to check the clover patch before I come home, Sarah

With a steady determination, she slung the bridle over one shoulder, and lugged the cumbersome rope with the other. Trudging down the slope, she half carted, half dragged the heavy burden, hoping and praying Stormy was grazing contentedly in his favorite runaway spot. As she approached the creek, she heard an odd rushing sound, like a giant fan blowing madly. The trees lining the bank blocked her view and, it wasn't until she cleared the tree line, that she understood the strange sound. The once gently trickling creek had become a fast flowing torrent crashing over the smooth stones, with wild foaming bubbles flooding the bank, engulfing the shrubs and plants. Sarah watched the red muddy current, uneasy and uncertain. How could one rainstorm turn a babbling brook into a raging monster? Surely Blackie didn't cross this or did she? It would certainly explain the condition she was in. *Maybe if I call Stormy he can get across, too.* Mustering her loudest bellow she called, **"STORMY! STORMY!"** and waited, but the rushing water was a soundproof wall. *I guess I'll have to go after him.* Walking down to the squishy embankment, she decided to leave her tennis shoes on and clinging to a low hanging branch, she lowered her foot into the stream. But the current was too swift, and it nearly yanked her shoe off. She gulped. "I'll be washed away for sure." If only there was a bridge, but Virgil had never built one. *I need something to hang on to! The rope! Maybe I can wade across using the rope!*

Finding a sturdy tree trunk, Sarah tied one end of the rope around it and the other end around her waist. *Just in case I slip, the rope will keep me from going far,* she reassured herself. Now came the hardest part; edging into the cold swirling water. Clinging to the rope so tightly, her hands felt glued in place, she slid down, her teeth chattering, as she sank deep into the chilly water. Once she gained a foothold, she realized she'd have to back across to keep the rope taut. "One step at a time. Help me get across this creek, Lord."

She was progressing slowly but steadily when a large rock upstream worked its way loose, suddenly striking her ankle, the icy water sharpening the pain. Crying out at the unexpected pang, she lost her balance and sank below like a sack of potatoes. The rope fell out of her hand, and she flailed her arms aimlessly. With her sore ankle throbbing, she kicked and fought to pull herself the surface. Felling like a rubber ball, she bounced from rock to rock before landing on a huge boulder. Grabbing at it, she clung tightly and clawed her way to the top, coughing and sputtering. From her slippery perch, she examined herself, thankful there were no serious injuries, just some scrapes.

Now she was very close to the other side with only a few feet remaining. To her amazement, three round stepping stones provided a safe passage through the sudsing whirl. Creeping down the boulder, she made it across, wet a little bruised, and very muddy, but intact. *Thank you, God,* she panted, untying the rope from around her waist and securing it to the nearest tree. The alfalfa patch wasn't far; only a small hike through the woods that now resembled a rain forest. Taking a breath as if she was swimming underwater, Sarah dove into the scratchy underbrush as twigs and branches reached out, clawing her face and hands. The once clear trail crawled with weeds and vines, their long wiggly arms entwining around her legs, determined to drag her down and devour her. All the while, strange bitter tasting bugs flew in her mouth, and thirsty mosquitoes feasted on her exposed flesh. Despite her thrashing, coughing, spitting, and itching, Sarah managed to hear a sound that wasn't her own. It caught her by surprise, and she stood frozen, hoping to hear it again. There it was again! "Stormy, Stormy, where are you?" she called out. The afternoon sun was low in the sky, leaving a dim shadowy light filtering through the leafy branches. With the shadows, playing tricks on her eyes, it took a few moments to focus, but suddenly, almost directly in front of her, a black form struggled desperately in the entanglement. Forgetting her bruises and scratches, Sarah plunged ahead through the bristling underbrush calling out to the exhausted pony. "I'm here, boy, I'm here," she said, finally reaching him.

Stormy answered with a low, weak whinny.

"What's the matter, boy? Are you stuck in all these brambles? Don't worry, I'll get you out." Clearing the web of vines from around his feet, she stared for a second in disbelief. Then realizing the horrible truth, she cried out, *"Oh no! Who could do such a thing?"* A rusty trap had snapped cruelly around his fetlock, the steel jaws piercing unmercifully deeper each time Stormy tried to free himself. Sarah's eyes brimmed with tears, her heart in agony. *How could anyone use such a cruel instrument of torture on innocent trusting animals?* Forcing herself to be calm for Stormy's sake, she delicately cleared away the tangled brush. "Hold still, boy. I have to figure out how to get you out of this thing." Careful not to cut herself on the rusted teeth, she grabbed two sturdy sticks and pried the vicious mouth open. Then nudging his side with her head, Stormy lifted his injured hoof from the bloodthirsty trap.

After removing the knotted brush from over his head, she slipped his bridle on and led the hobbling pony slowly back to the creek. He was weak and tired, and Sarah wondered if he had the strength to cross the still angry creek. *Okay, Lord. We've made it this far, but we still have a ways to go. I really hate to keep bugging You, but could You please help us get back? I sure have been praying a lot, lately, but like Virgil said, You're always here for us, and I sure am glad.*

Facing that creek, Sarah was frightened. It was one thing to go it alone, but it was quite another to try and lead a crippled pony across. But she couldn't let Stormy feel her fear because he might not follow her. This was definitely a test of her trust. "Well, boy, we might as well get started before it gets too dark." Since wet reins were as slippery as a lathered bar of soap, she tied the rope to Stormy's halter and waded forward, coaxing him to follow. Limping to the edge, he sniffed the water and took a drink. Then he paused. "Come on, Stormy. You can do it!" Inching his way down, he crashed in and stumbled before gaining his balance. "Good boy. Don't worry. That happened to me, too."

Each slow step was an effort, and she winced every time she heard a hoof hit a rock or slide against one. "This cold water's good for your leg," she told him. "It'll make the swelling go down some and clean out your cuts. When we get home, David will call the vet, and we'll get you and Blackie fixed up in no time. You'll see." Talking to him cut the tension and when they finally reached the other side, Stormy leaped onto the bank with a loud heaving groan. "The worst part is over now. Thank you, God," she said looking up. The sun was floating lower and lower like a popped balloon sinking slowly to the ground, and she wondered what time it was. Limping back to the barn, she hoped she wasn't in too much trouble.

At last, the barn came into view, and she saw David peering through his new binoculars. He saw her and waved, then hiked down to meet her. "Sarah, what's happened? Are you hurt?"

"I'm okay, but Stormy and Blackie need a vet."

"Here, give me that rope. You both look exhausted."

"I am kind of tired, but I couldn't go home without looking for Stormy. Are you and Mom mad?"

"No, but we were worried when we came home from the hospital and you weren't home. So we drove back and found the note you left. What happened to Stormy?"

"After you left, Blackie came home all scratched and cut, and I just knew something wasn't right, so I went looking for Stormy and he was caught in an awful trap.

"And you got him out of it?"

"Just barely, but the hardest part was crossing that flooded creek." Catching her breath, she exclaimed, "How is Virgil? With so much happening, I almost forgot to ask."

"He's badly hurt, and he'll be in the hospital for a while, but with a lot of rest, the doctors said he should recover."

"That's a relief," she sighed wearily. It seemed like years had passed since she found Virgil, so much had happened.

Shortly after Stormy was secured in a stall, the vet's gray van roared up the drive with Linda following behind in her car. As Dr. Thompson came forward and greeted everyone, he reminded Sarah of a big burly lumberjack with his copper colored hair, neatly trimmed beard and hazel green eyes. He even wore a plaid shirt. After inquiring about Virgil, he turned his attention to the reason of his visit. "I understand we have some injured ponies."

"Yes," said Sarah, walking coldly past Linda into the barn. "They both ran away during the storm. Blackie came back on her own, but Stormy was caught in a trap across the creek."

"You crossed that swollen creek by yourself?" asked Dr. Thompson, his bushy eyebrows arched high in surprise.

Sarah blushed and answered modestly, "Well, yes, but it was scary. I slipped and fell, but I had a rope tied to a tree and around my waist."

"Smart thinking, young lady."

"She's done a lot of smart thinking today, and we're very proud of her," beamed Mrs. Conner, as she and Linda came into the barn with a tray of sandwiches and drinks.

Sarah grabbed two sandwiches and ate them hungrily, while Dr. Thompson examined the ponies. "They're both pretty banged up, but Stormy's foreleg is the most serious. They're both going to need treatments several times a day."

"I'll do it!" volunteered Sarah.

"I can't burden you with that, Sarah," said Linda. "I'll hire someone. It will be safer that way."

"I'm not afraid of Blackie or Stormy." Sarah shot back. "They know me and trust me."

"What do you think, Dr. Thompson?" asked David.

"I see no reason why Sarah can't handle the work. I've treated these ponies for years, and they are both gentle animals. Remember the night Stormy was born, Linda? What a night that was."

"Yes, I remember. There was a terrible storm that night, too."

"Is that how Stormy got his name?" asked Sarah.

"It sure is. Poor Stormy had a rude awakening when he stood on his wobbly legs for the first time," said Dr. Thompson, fondly scratching Stormy's ears.

"What happened?" asked Sarah.

"A bolt of lightning lit up the sky. It looked like daytime for a few seconds. And then came the loudest boom of thunder I've ever heard. It knocked poor Stormy to his knees. He was too scared to stand, and Blackie was too nervous to nurse. Virgil and I stayed out here most of the night settling them down."

"So that's why he ran away during this storm. He's still afraid of lightning and thunder," reasoned Sarah.

"That's right. I always supply Virgil with a few mild tranquilizers each spring for these summer storms, but this time he wasn't able to give him one because of the accident. I do the same thing for a lot of dog owners, too. Otherwise, Stormy's a well-mannered pony with a spunky personality. Well, what's it gonna be folks? Is Sarah going to take care of these critters or not?"

"It's fine with me. Honey, how about you?" asked David.

"It's fine with me, too, if it suits Linda."

Linda had been unusually quiet during Dr. Thompson's explanation, but she agreed to let Sarah care for the ponies. Then she added, "I still can't help being afraid."

"Under the circumstances, it's perfectly understandable," said Dr. Thompson softly, before changing the subject. "These two have suffered sprains in addition to their cuts and scrapes. I'm going to give them an injection to help fight any infection that might set in. Then, I'll show you what to do, Sarah, for the next week.

Dr. Thompson cleaned the wounds with a mild, soapy mixture. Then he clipped the hair around Stormy's pastern and applied a poultice. As he wrapped the foreleg with a fresh bandage, he said, "You'll have to change this dressing once a day."

"That doesn't look too hard," replied Sarah, paying close attention to the procedure.

"This is the easiest part. There's quite a bit more work involved with the sprains."

He continued with the final stage of treatment. "These sprains require a warm compress applied three times a day. You'll need a bucket of lukewarm saltwater by your side." Dr. Thompson demonstrated by dipping a piece of clean cloth into a bucket of tepid water. Then he wrung it out and wrapped it around each sprained leg.

"Leave this on for twenty minutes. Then you apply this paste over the swollen areas and this ointment on the scrapes. Now you practice while I watch."

Blackie had two sprains and numerous scrapes and cuts, and Sarah felt clumsy wrapping the wet bandage around her foreleg, but by the third try, she proved to be fairly efficient.

"Since they'll be recuperating in their stalls, give them a hot bran mash instead of oats. The only time they can be moved is when the stalls are being cleaned. Cleanliness and rest are essential," Dr. Thompson added as he packed his bag.

"How much do I owe you?" asked Linda, reaching for her purse.

"Nothing right now. Your father has an account with me. All he needs is this bill."

"Thank you, Dr. Thompson. I'll put it on his desk."

"I'll be back in a couple days to check on everything. If you have any questions, Sarah, give me a call," he said, as he left.

"You have your work cut out for you. Are you sure you can handle it?" asked her mother.

"Sure, Mom, I'll be fine."

Linda excused herself and went into the tack room to place the bill on Virgil's desk. A moment later, there was a muffled shriek from within. Sarah and her parents ran to the door where Linda was reading the newspaper clippings left on the desk, her face as white as a sheet.

Chapter Ten

Making Amends

"Where did these come from?" she stammered.

"I, I, was looking for your phone number, and they were in the drawer. I wasn't snooping, honest," mumbled Sarah.

"I just can't believe this. I'm so shocked!" exclaimed Linda, sitting down and shaking her head.

"What is it, Linda?" asked Mrs. Conner.

"These articles. Look." Handing the clippings to Amy and David, they quickly read them and returned them to the desk, their faces saddened.

Linda shuddered, then buried her face in her hands. "I never knew it was my own father who saved that child. I thought he was wasting his time at another silly auction. Why didn't he tell me?" she wept. "All these years I've been blaming him for my mother's death."

"It's not too late for you to make amends," comforted Mrs. Conner.

"What if he had died today? I'd have been angry at him for the rest of my life."

"God's given you this opportunity to start fresh," said David kindly.

Looking up, her eyes wet and bright, Linda said, "You're right. What's happened today is no coincidence."

"Virgil says the Lord works in mysterious ways," offered Sarah meekly.

"He certainly does," agreed Linda with a weak smile. "Sarah, I'm sorry for all the trouble I caused you."

"That's okay. It all makes sense, now."

"I think I'll go back to the hospital. I want to be there when Dad wakes up."

"Don't worry, Linda. If Sarah needs any help out here, we'll take care of it," said David.

"Thank you. You've all been so kind," she sniffed, rising to leave. I'll call Ginny this evening and let her know what's happened. She's not going to believe her ears."

For the next week, Sarah dutifully cared for Stormy and Blackie. Between treatments, she tended to the damaged garden, set the damp tack and hay out to dry and even managed to milk Dolly. There was always something to do, and she went home every evening feeling tired but pleased with the progress both she and the ponies were making. On the third day, Linda came by with a batch of homemade chocolate chip cookies.

"They're my favorite," said Sarah, with her mouth full.

"I'm glad you like them. Take the rest home."

"Thanks! My Mom won't bake in the summer because it makes the house too hot."

"I don't blame her, but it's the least I could do after all the trouble I caused you."

"You didn't cause *that* much trouble," joked Sarah, "but I was pretty mad at you!"

"I know I made things pretty uncomfortable for you and your parents."

Sarah reflected a moment, then said, "If I had seen my mother killed by a horse, I'd probably send that horse straight to the glue factory."

"I asked my father to sell Stormy so many times, but he was so attached to him, he just couldn't. Then I started to blame him for what happened. I accused him of all kinds of hateful things, like loving his animals more than my mother. After I left for college, I hardly ever came home," explained Linda, gazing across the open fields. "He had a beard all his life, so yesterday, after he came out of surgery, I said, 'I know why you shaved your beard, Dad.' You should have seen the look on his face."

"I guess it wasn't anyone's fault, was it?" asked Sarah.

"You're absolutely right. And I let my resentment eat away at my heart, like a poison. Anyway, I'm awfully glad you left those clippings on the desk. It helped me realize the truth, along with what Dr. Thompson said."

"Did Virgil ever visit the family?"

"He wanted that family to thank God, not him, so he never came forward.

"Why didn't he ever tell you what happened?"

"I asked him that last night, and he said he was responsible and no reason, no matter how good, could ever make up for him forgetting to put Stormy in his stall before he left that day."

"Poor Virgil. He must be so sad on the inside, but he's always so happy on the outside," remarked Sarah.

"I told him that it was just as wrong to blame himself, but I think it will take a while for him to forgive himself," sighed Linda. Wiping a tear from her eye, she smiled and asked, "And how are our two patients doing today?"

"Oh, they're improving every day. They still limp, but most of the swelling has gone down. Come on, I'll show you," said Sarah, forgetting Linda was still afraid of horses.

From the outside of the stall, Linda watched as she changed Stormy's dressing. "I need to clean out their stalls, now. Could you lead Blackie out for me?"

"Well, uh, I'll try," she stammered.

"Don't be afraid. She's just like an old puppy dog," encouraged Sarah.

As Linda cautiously led Blackie outside, she choked out, "She remembers me."

"Well, of course she does. She loves you," chirped Sarah, following behind. "She's probably been wondering where you've been all these years!"

"I'm sorry, Blackie. I missed you, too," cooed Linda, as she lovingly brushed her devoted pony.

"I tried training her to show, but she's too old now," said Sarah.

"She performed perfectly in the ring for many years. She's earned her retirement. I think it's time to concentrate on you know who," said Linda, pointing to Stormy, "once he's fit to ride."

"You mean you'll help me train Stormy?" blubbered Sarah.

"If it's all right with your parents, I'll do the best I can."

"After Dr. Thompson explained everything, they said I could ride him when he's well, except on rainy days!" laughed Sarah.

"I'm so glad. I know Dad will be thrilled to hear it."

"When will I be able to visit Virgil? I really miss him," asked Sarah.

"How about tomorrow afternoon? Say around four o'clock."

"For real?"

"Sure. He's been asking about you every day. I'll pick you up at your house."

The next day, Sarah hurried home from the farm to get cleaned up in time for Linda. As much as she wanted to see Virgil, she felt strange and nervous and couldn't get used to the idea of Virgil lying in a hospital bed.

"How should I act? What should I say?" she asked her mother.

"Just be yourself, and it'll be fine," reassured her mother.

Virgil was sitting up in bed reading a magazine when they entered his room. A white bandage circled his shaved head, and Sarah thought he looked pale and thin despite the grin of pleasure on his face. "Come give ol' Virgil a hug," he said, holding out his right arm.

"Oh, Virgil, I didn't think they were ever going to let me come see you," she exclaimed, her fears dissolving like a swallowed pill. "And so much has happened, I don't know where to begin," she said, settling herself on the edge of his bed, while Linda sat in the chair.

"Before ya git started, I gotta thank ya most dearly fer saving my life. I mighta been a goner if you and Duke hadn't come along when ya did."

As he spoke, she noticed his speech was slightly slurred and much slower. Blushing, she replied, "I was pretty scared when I found you."

"I heerd ya praying over me, but I couldn't answer back. Both me and Stormy are ever grateful to ya, missy."

"I hope you don't mind that I told Dad about Stormy's rescue," said Linda. "You'll have to fill him in on the details, though." Sarah tried to tell Virgil everything during the short time she was allowed to visit and just as she was finishing, a nice nurse politely informed them that visiting hours were over.

"When are you coming home?" she asked, as they prepared to leave.

"Them doctors can't make up their minds about me," chuckled Virgil, "but Linda will tell ya as soon as we know. You come visit me again, real soon."

"I'll bring her back next week, Dad," promised Linda, kissing her father goodbye.

Sarah gave him a quick hug, noticing again that he didn't lift his left arm. As they walked quietly down the clean white corridors and out the heavy glass doors, Linda asked, "Are you feeling okay?"

"What's the matter with him?" she blurted out. "I though he just had a bad bump on his head!"

"He did have a bad bump; a bump so bad it caused a stroke," explained Linda.

"What's a stroke?"

"A stroke can be mild or serious and fortunately for us, his was mild. When the beam hit his head, tiny blood vessels in his brain broke and that's why his speech is slurry."

"Is that why he can only move one arm?" asked Sarah, her voice cracking.

"Yes, he has trouble moving his left side."

"Can he walk?"

"Yes, but only for a short distance because he's shaky and tires easily."

"Sarah's throat tightened when she asked, "Will he ever get well?"

"He should make a full recovery, but it will take many weeks of rest and therapy. These things take time to heal," explained Linda gently.

Tears welled up in Sarah's eyes.

"You've been a big comfort to him. His mind's at ease knowing you're caring for the ponies so well, and that's important to his recovery. And there's one more thing I should tell you," added Linda.

"I hope it's not bad," she sniffed.

"No, I think you'll like this. I've decided to move back home."

"You are? Oh, Linda, that'll be great having you there all the time! When?"

"This weekend. It won't take long, since most of the furniture in my apartment belongs to my roommate."

"I bet Virgil's happy about that.

"He sure is and with Ginny and me taking care of him, he'll get well in a hurry!" she laughed. "And while

Dad's still in the hospital, you and I can keep each other company."

"Don't you have to go to work?" asked Sarah.

"Not until school starts in September," replied Linda with a sly wink.

"You mean you're a teacher?" she gulped.

"How'd you guess? Yes, I'm the new seventh grade science teacher at the middle school. You might even be a student of mine!"

"I'm afraid science isn't one of my better subjects," admitted Sarah sheepishly.

"If I'm your teacher, it will be one of your favorite subjects, I guarantee!" declared Linda, pulling up in front of Sarah's house. "Don't forget, Dr. Thompson is coming out tomorrow morning at eight thirty," she reminded, as Sarah bounded up the porch steps.

"I'll be there at eight sharp!" she said, waving good-bye.

*   *   *

As Dr. Thompson made his usual silent examination, Sarah waited anxiously. When he finally finished, he stood up and announced, "They're making excellent progress."

"When can I ride Stormy?" she asked hopefully.

"Not for another two or three weeks, at least."

Her heart sank. July would be over in three weeks. "Is there any chance he'll be well enough to enter in the Labor Day Show?"

"That's asking a lot of this little fella, considering what he's been through," said Dr. Thompson, gravely.

"Sarah, we don't want Stormy to risk a permanent injury," reminded Linda.

"I'd give up riding forever rather than making him limp the rest of his life. It's just that I was hoping so hard he might have a chance."

"I should be able to give you a definite answer in a couple weeks," said Dr. Thompson. "If he continues to improve the way he has so far, I'd say he has a fifty-fifty chance."

"You hear that, Stormy? We might make it after all!"

"Continue the treatments and add a slow, short walk. We gotta keep those legs from stiffening up now that the swelling is down. Keep up the good work, Sarah. You're doing a terrific job," he encouraged.

*   *   *

Two weeks later, he returned and watched intensely as Sarah led each pony around the yard. Then he examined them slowly, making her tense with anticipation. *I wish he'd say something!* she agonized.

"What do you think, doctor?" asked Linda, shattering the silence.

"I want to watch Stormy trot," was his grim faced answer.

Jogging around the yard, Sarah was seasick with worry. *Please let him be well, God.*

"I've seen enough, Sarah. You can stop now."

After the longest ten minutes of her life passed, he turned to then and smiled. "I see no reason why he can't be shown in the halter and pleasure classes. Save the strenuous events for the spring show. No figure eights or hind quarter turns for now."

Her heart did back flips at the sound of this good news. Then she breathed a quiet prayer of thanks. "Don't worry, Dr. Thompson. We'll be extra careful with him."

"Will you be at the show this year?" inquired Linda.

"Yes, I'm the on duty vet, so I'll be watching for you. You've got a good coach, Sarah. Listen to her and you'll be a winner!" he said, giving Linda a smile.

Chapter Eleven

Show Day

With just over a month to train, there wasn't much time to prepare, but she and Linda practiced diligently six days a week, with everyone resting on Sunday. Training for the halter class proved harder than she expected since Stormy wavered to and fro like a car skidding on ice when it was time to trot. Even at a walk, he was like a toddler; easily distracted and always wanting to nibble on a blade of grass! He resisted the drills and stubbornly refused to line up his legs squarely, giving Sarah a backache each night from the constant lifting and placing of each hoof in its proper place.

She looked forward to practicing for the pleasure class, since she could ride for that. But much of Linda's attention was devoted to equitation, and she was much stricter than Virgil had been. "Heads up! Hands and heels down! Back straight!" she would say as Sarah and Stormy went round and round the mended corral. "Every part of the body has a special place," she repeated, and if Sarah moved an inch, Linda saw it and corrected her immediately.

After an exasperating two weeks, Sarah was worn out and irritable. "I don't think we're good enough," she complained, collapsing on a bale of straw. "We need more time."

"We'll make it, you'll see. In another week or so, everything will fall into place," she encouraged.

"I don't know. Stormy won't pay attention to any of my commands or cues."

"More is sinking into that brain of his than you realize. Try to be patient. The first few shows are the hardest because you and the horse are still learning and gaining experience. Let's take a break from the heat and go inside. I want to show you something."

"What is it?"

"My first show outfit." From the attic, Linda had retrieved a dusty cardboard box. From it, she lifted out a pair of small faded chaps. "I found this box last night. I had forgotten that my mother saved these."

"They look pretty good, considering how old they are – whoops! Sorry, I didn't mean you were old!" Sarah cringed with embarrassment.

"It's okay, I know what you meant," she chuckled. "Take a look at this hat."

Out of a smaller box came a well preserved cowgirl hat. It had once been white as new fallen snow, but over the years it had dimmed in the oven-like attic. As they reminisced through old photo albums, Sarah felt more encouraged. "You'll be competing in the junior class with other riders ages 17 and under, just like I did," explained Linda.

"Do you think I stand a chance of winning?"

"Focus on doing your very best rather than winning. You'll have a better time and will learn more from your mistakes."

"But I don't want to make any mistakes," protested Sarah.

"There's nothing wrong with making an honest mistake. That's how you improve and gain confidence. I started showing when I was seven on an old plow horse, but I didn't win anything till I was ten. And it was far from first place. Some of the junior riders have had years of experience and for others, it will be their first time, too. So you have nothing to worry about."

"I'll try to remember, but the closer the show gets, the more nervous I get!"

"That's normal, too," smiled Linda.

*   *   *

A week later, still discouraged, but resolving not to quit, Sarah gave Stormy the same voice and hand signals for squaring up his hooves. Expecting his usual response, she nearly fell over when he lined up each hoof perfectly and stood quietly. "Good boy!" she praised him over and over, giving him extra carrot chunks. "Did you see him?" she shouted to Linda.

"I sure did! It's about time, Stormy," applauded Linda from the top railing.

"It's just like you said. He's finally getting the idea!" she exclaimed.

"With Stormy, I think it's a matter of who's more stubborn, you or him!"

"Stormy, you're a character, you know that?" said Sarah fondly.

"Now we can load him in the trailer and drive to the show grounds to practice," suggested Linda.

"So he can get used to a new ring?"

"Exactly. We'll go every day until the show."

"Do you think Virgil will be out of the hospital in time?"

"I wish I knew, but the doctors can't say for certain."

"I bet he's tired of being cooped up in that room all day," mused Sarah.

"Cabin fever is definitely setting in! He's getting ornery and starting to complain which is a sure sign he's on the mend.

Sarah laughed. It wasn't hard to picture Virgil driving the nurses crazy with his stories and tall tales. But then, her smile faded at the thought of him missing their first show.

With Labor Day only a week away, the last minute details popped up like weeds after a rain. Besides practicing, much time was devoted to grooming and polishing tack and then the truck and trailer had to be scrubbed inside out!

The day before the show, Mrs. Conner said to Sarah, "Ask Linda to come have dinner with us this evening."

"Okay, Mom," she said, on her way out the door.

When the two arrived that evening, Sarah was surprised. Steaks were grilling, rather than the usual hamburgers. "Wow, Mom, what's the occasion?"

"As I recall, you like to have steak on your birthday, isn't that right?" quipped her mother.

"My birthday!" she gasped.

"You forgot, you forgot!" squealed Allison in delight.

"Wait a minute! My birthday's tomorrow. On show day!" she sputtered. "I did forget. I can't believe it!"

"Well, we didn't," said David, coming down the hall with an armful of presents. "And because tomorrow is such a busy day, we thought it best to celebrate a little early."

After a delicious dinner of steak, fresh picked corn on the cob, rolls, salad, cake and ice cream, Sarah admired the four presents, all wrapped in horsey wrapping paper, wondering which one to open first.

"Open mine first! I wrapped it myself!" said Allison bouncing on the couch.

"I can tell!" she joked, as she selected the sloppily wrapped gift.

"Hurry up!"

"Okay, okay," said Sarah with growing excitement. She hadn't even asked for anything and wondered what she'd gotten. Allison's gift took her completely by surprise; a large framed photograph of herself and Stormy. "When did you take this picture of us?"

"It wasn't easy," said David, "but Linda offered to take secret snapshots of you two. It was all Allison's idea. She picked out the frame and paid for the enlargement with her allowance."

"Thank you, Allison. This is the nicest gift you've ever given me," she said, hugging her squirming sister. Turning to Linda, Sarah teased good naturedly, "I usually get a Barbie doll that *she* wants."

"She had one picked out this year, too, but she was willing to sacrifice this time," laughed Mrs. Conner. "Why don't you open Linda's next?" she added.

Linda handed Sarah a deep square shaped box. ""I hope you like it."

"You didn't have to get me anything," she blushed. "You've already given me tons of free riding lessons."

"If it hadn't been for you, I'd still be afraid of the sweetest ponies in Kentucky. And I've enjoyed our lessons so much, I thought I'd advertise for a few more students."

As Sarah listened, she opened the box and lifted the lid. "It's, it's beautiful," she stammered, taking the cream-colored cowgirl hat out of the box for all to see and admire.

"I hope it fits. I couldn't sneak up and measure your head, so your mother loaned me your old straw hat."

"That's what I was going to wear," said Sarah, placing the velvety hat on her head as if it were a fragile piece of glass. "It feels like a perfect fit!"

"And it looks perfect on you!" complimented Linda.

"It certainly does," agreed her mother, "But remember it's only for show days."

"I'll keep it in the box, like Linda does."

"Which one next?" asked Allison breathless with anticipation.

"You'd think it was her birthday!" laughed Sarah.

"I *love* opening presents, even if they aren't mine!" she giggled.

"This one's from Aunt Betsy and Uncle Burton," read Sarah, picking up another large box. This birthday was going from wonderful to fabulous as she removed a shiny pair of black leather cowgirl boots. Speechless with delight and disbelief, she yanked off her tennis shoes, slid the sleek boots on, clomped around the house and then announced, "They feel great!"

"You can call your Aunt Betsy and Uncle Burton this evening and thank them," reminded her mother.

"That's a relief, because I hate writing thank-you notes."

"And then you can follow up your phone call with a thank you note after the show," said Mrs. Conner with her Miss Manners expression.

"Okay," she groaned happily.

"Next one, please!" pleaded Allison.

"For heaven's sake, open the last box before your sister has a conniption fit!" said David, shaking his head. "I don't get it. She knows what's inside."

"As long as the birthday girl doesn't know, that's all that matters," explained Mrs. Conner.

"This looks like a clothes box. Sounds like one, too," she surmised, after shaking the rectangular shaped gift. Just as she guessed, four pieces of western attire were neatly arranged inside the tissue-lined box: a burgundy shirt with a beige ruffle, blue jeans and blue gray chaps that complimented a blue and burgundy hatband hidden underneath the ensemble.

"Thanks Mom and Dad. This is the best birthday I've ever had!" Sarah stopped abruptly as she realized, *Hey, I called David, Dad. I wonder if he noticed.* Glancing his way, he winked at her and smiled warmly. *He noticed! That's funny. It seemed so natural.*

And here's a card from Grandma," her mother said, breaking through her thoughts.

"Fifty dollars! Wow! Can I call Grandma, too?"

"She's going to be calling you in about an hour," confided her mother.

"I just can't believe all these presents. It's everything I needed."

"We wanted you to look terrific for the show!" said David.

"And you'll feel more confident, knowing how well you look," added Linda. "Well, I better be on my way. We've got a full day tomorrow, so get a good night's sleep."

That night, Sarah was too excited to sleep as all the tiny details of the following day invaded her mind like ants at a picnic. Brushing away the pushy thoughts proved futile, since more arrived to take their place, so she opened her book on the nightstand, but after reading the same page over three times, she gave up and turned off the light. *I'll never get to sleep!*

The next thing she heard was her radio alarm clock playing one of her favorite songs, so she snuggled in bed and listened to it before facing the day – *Show Day! It was here. It was really here!*

"Think you can eat something this morning," greeted her mother cheerfully.

"I don't think so, Mom."

"I figured as much so here's a couple sandwiches for later. Try to drink a glass of milk, at least."

"Okay." Sarah sipped slowly and managed to force down half a glass without throwing up.

David drove her to the farm where they found Linda in the barn gathering all the supplies needed for each event.

"All this for one pony?" asked David.

"Yes, Dad, it's all very important," giggled Sarah. "We have to groom him constantly."

"He can't have a speck of dust on him. Those judges have eyes like a hawk," Linda emphasized, as they all helped load the equipment into the trailer. "Now it's Stormy's turn."

Sarah led him up the ramp as she had done for the past week. He followed sleepily, as though this day was no different from any of the others. "I wish I was as calm as you are, boy."

"He'll perk up when he sees all the activity at the show grounds," said Linda. "I think that's everything. Ready or not, here we come!"

"We'll see you there," said David, opening the truck door for Sarah. "Don't worry about feeling nervous. Just do your best, and remember you're already a winner in our eyes!"

"Thanks, Dad, I'll try," she said swallowing another pesky lump.

When they arrived, she backed Stormy out of the trailer and tried to practice for the halter class, but he was too distracted by the noisy creak of trailers, the smell and whinnies of excited horses and the shouts of children filling the fairgrounds. "Stormy, pay attention to me!" she scolded.

"Sarah, don't get upset. He needs time to get used to the new surroundings. Don't forget, this is his first show, too. Why don't you two stroll around for a while and I'll go sign in."

"I'm sorry, Stormy. I didn't mean to yell at you. You wanna go for a little walk?"

As they wove through the maze of trailers, Sarah noticed a few large expensive looking setups but most were plain and average like Virgil's. There were lots of different breeds tied up, from tall lanky Thoroughbreds and stocky Quarter horses to majestic Arabians with flowing silvery manes to tiny fuzzy Shetland ponies. All were munching hay, and Sarah was somewhat relieved to see that most of the competition were ordinary pets with riders near her own age. Soon, Stormy lost interest and settled down, preferring to graze. Feeling calmer, she realized how hungry she'd become and dug into her knapsack to find the sandwiches. She tried practicing for the halter class again and was grateful when Stormy squared his hooves perfectly. "Good boy! Now please remember to do that in the ring!"

"Sarah, it's time to get dressed," chimed Linda, taking her outfit off the hanger.

"Already? Are my parents here yet?"

"They've got front row seats. See? There's your mom and Allison waving to us."

"Where's my Dad?"

"Oh, he's probably gone to get something to drink."

Sarah had been dressed for only ten minutes when she heard the announcer call for the junior halter class. "You're number nine," reminded Linda, pinning the paper to her back.

"I think I'm going to be sick," she answered hoarsely.

"Just pretend you're back at our own rinky-dink corral," coached Linda.

"Okay," she said, shivering.

Once in the show ring, she tried to do as Linda said, but everything was a blur. She felt clumsy and awkward, as if she and everyone else were moving in slow motion. And suddenly, it was over and before she knew what was happening, she found herself filing out with all the rest of the losers where Linda was waiting for her.

"You did just fine!" she beamed

"I don't even know what I did or didn't do," lamented Sarah.

"Not to worry. I took a video of you."

"I can't wait to see myself!"

"You'll have to wait because we don't have much time to get ready for the pleasure class. I'll give him a quick brushing, and you put his bridle on," said Linda, giving Sarah last-minute instructions. "Now remember, the judge will be watching you very closely, so pay attention to your equitation. Head up, heels low, back straight, and a light easy rein. But don't stiffen up. You're not a robot."

Sarah mounted, repeating Linda's reminders under her breath, and nudged Stormy into the ring. This time her surroundings came into focus as she and the other riders walked briskly around the ring. It was a fairly large class, and the judge took his time viewing each contestant before giving the signal to trot. Jogging around the ring, she stopped worrying about the other riders and concentrated on herself. Soon, she forgot about them completely and rode confidently as if she and Stormy were the only ones in the ring. Finally, the judge signaled or a lope. Stormy broke into his easy going canter and changed leads smoothly when asked to reverse. Then the judge called for another jog followed by a final walk. He finished writing his notes and walked over to the announcer, handing him the folded paper. A woman holding a tray with six large ribbons and three trophies walked to the center of the ring with the judge and photographer. For a moment, Sarah forgot her number and had to wrench her neck around to get a glimpse of the black number nine plastered against her sweaty back. Her heart was pounding hard now, that it was nearly over. "Number nine, number nine," she pleaded under her breath as the announcer's voice boomed over the loudspeaker.

"With such a large class of excellent riders, it was a tough decision for our judge. But as you know, there can only be six official winners, so let us begin. Our sixth place winner is number twelve, Comanche, owned and ridden by Shelly Jenkins."

The audience clapped as Shelly rode forward and accepted her purple ribbon, posing for a snapshot. "Fifth place is awarded to number two, Pepper, owned and ridden by Thomas Kirk."

Sarah's heart began to sink. *I'm not good enough to compete with these other kids if I can't even get sixth or fifth place.*

"Fourth place goes to …" but the announcer's voice faded from her ears. Another girl, a teenager, riding a golden Palomino rode forward to accept the yellow ribbon. *This is taking forever*, she thought, trying not to squirm in her saddle.

"And now it's time to give away some trophies," sang the announcer. "Our third place winner is number nine, Stormy, owned and ridden by Sarah Taylor."

"What? Did he say number nine?" she asked the rider to her left, who smiled and nodded. Feeling as if she'd been struck by lightning, Sarah nudged Stormy forward to accept the white ribbon with gold lettering and a small but sparkling trophy. She posed for her picture hoping her grin didn't look too goofy, but then again, *who cares? I won third place!*

Scanning the crowd, she laughed out loud when she saw her family with Linda, jumping up and down, clapping and waving. After the last two awards were presented, she rode out of the ring, the sound of clapping still lingering in her ears.

"My sister won third place," she heard Allison bragging as she rode up to greet her fans.

"You were wonderful, Sarah!" cried her mother, through a whir of photos.

"Thanks, Mom! I can hardly believe it myself. But where's Dad? Didn't he come?"

"I wouldn't have missed this for the world!" she heard him say from the other side of the trailer.

"Neither would I!" came another familiar voice.

Dismounting, Sarah ran around the trailer to find David pushing Virgil in a wheelchair. "You brought Virgil to see me! Are you well enough to go home?"

"They let me out on good behavior!" chuckled Virgil.

"You were driving them crazy is more like it!" teased Linda, giving her father a kiss.

"That's enough about me, now. I want to give my congratulations to Sarah and Stormy here."

"How'd we look, Virgil?"

"You two were as smooth as fresh-churned butter!"

"The announcer made one mistake, though, she said.

"What's that? I don't recollect hearing nothin' outa the ordinary," asked Virgil, scratching his fuzzy white whiskers.

"He said I was Stormy's owner instead of you," she explained.

"Is that a fact? Well, them announcers just read what's put on the card, ain't that so, Linda?"

"That's right, Dad," answered Linda, trying to conceal a smile.

"I don't get it," replied Sarah.

"I reckon Stormy has a new owner!" declared Virgil, enthusiastically.

"Stormy belongs to me?" Sarah gasped in disbelief.

"That's what this here registration card says," he said, handing her the entry form.

"Oh, Stormy, you're mine, all mine," she exclaimed, burying her head in his thick lustrous mane. Then looking up, she blurted, "You were my dream horse all along!"

*　　　*　　　*

That night, Sarah lay in bed for a long time reflecting over the last few weeks and all that had happened. It was quite amazing to look back, and see how God had arranged all the pieces of this crazy puzzle. Everything fit together perfectly. Not only did she now understand Romans 8:28, she had actually experienced it in a very real and personal way. *All things really do work together for our good, if we love*

God and fit into His plans. Thank you, Lord, for working everything out so perfectly! Amen!

About the Author

Kathy Wilson was born in Tampa, Florida (a long time ago!) and moved to Wilmore, Kentucky in the 6th grade, where she got Toby, the horse of her dreams (a dream she really had in chapter two!) After graduating from Georgia Southern College, she became a military wife and got to travel the world. She now lives in Charleston, South Carolina and is retired from teaching middle school language arts. Other horse books by Kathy Wilson are Starshine's Shadow and Skylar's Special Summer.

Picture books by Ms. Wilson include Free to Good Home – A Christmas Tale, God Created It All!, Hair is Everywhere!, Not A Drop of Rain in Sight and The White Buck's World.

Made in the USA
Columbia, SC
04 November 2019

82681644R00100